The Last Converts of Christ

GIANCARLO GHEDINI

Copyright © 2025 by Giancarlo Ghedini
Story King Books
All rights reserved.

CONTENTS

PART ONE

The Innkeeper	2
Training	8
Two Roman Friends	11
A Dream	14
The Wealthy Spice Merchant	15
Two Thieves in a Tree	18
The Speech	20
How to Throw a Dagger	26
Another Dream	31
Brothers	33
Reason to Fear	39
Tour of the Palace	41
Family	44
The Spark	52
The Robbery	59
The Burial	65
Escape	67

PART TWO

The Doctor	76
Gratitude	79
The Pit	81
Number One Hundred	83
Palm Sunday	86
The Decision	90
Complaints	93
A Wound and an Argument	95
The Council of Thirteen	99
Seek and Find	107
A Story About Kezia	110
Rats	114
Divi Filius	116
Blessing vs the Blesser	119
Hope for the Hopeless	124
Passover	127
Rebel	130

The Lucky Three	134
The Trial of Thieves	136
The King Returns	141
Two Jesuses	145
Justice	151
Power	155
Second Chance	159

PART THREE

Golgotha	162
It Is Finished	170
Sweet Revenge	175
Resignation	179
Paradise	186
Following Orders	190
Old Friends	193
The Switch	198
Departing	203
Epilogue	206

ACKNOWLEDGMENTS

Special thanks to my good friend, Ryan Bohstedt.
Your pastoral insights and thoughts were most valuable.

For Jennifer.

PART ONE

The Innkeeper

The vineyard was still a dream. But the resolution to make it a reality came one violent morning shortly before the Passover festival began.

Nathan's inn was on a dirt road two miles outside of Jerusalem. It was a less-than-desirable area where schemers and honest men scraped to get by. There were gamblers and day laborers, beggars and thieves. Kezia and the boy woke to the sound of fighting outside the inn. Four large rogue tax collectors—outliers who'd abandoned their booths—were throwing a man to the ground, punching his face, kicking his side, and demanding he pay more money than he had.

Nathan had already dug a secret hole in the back room of the inn for Kezia and her son to hide, as prostitutes were sometimes abused under such circumstances. A small rug and table were fastened to a wooden trapdoor to cover the hole in the earthen floor. Kezia rushed her son to this hiding spot, threw her belongings in, and pulled the lid over the hole to cover themselves. They sat in the darkness and listened.

"Are you sure this is all you have?" asked Barak, with a fistful of Nathan's hair in his hand. Barak was the ringleader and largest of the tax collectors, though the other three men were not small.

"You gave us the same story last time," Barak went on, with breath that reeked of strong wine. "You finally found some extra money lying around in the end. Do we have to do this every single time? Let's go inside, shall we?"

Barak dragged Nathan by the back of his tunic along the dirt pathway leading to the inn's front door. It was already open. He threw the innkeeper to the ground.

Nathan's modest inn was made of stone and mud bricks and had a thatch roof. Aside from the food preparation and eating areas, there were four small rooms for travelers to stay. Kezia and the boy were the only permanent residents and lived in the back room with the secret hole in the ground. Due to the festival, the remaining three rooms were occupied by visiting families from the surrounding regions. By this time, they were all waking up to the sound of the innkeeper's harassment. One of the husbands staying there came out to defend Nathan. But when he saw Barak, accompanied by three other men almost as big, he had a change of heart and stayed in his room.

"You play knucklebones, don't you?" asked Barak. "Win anything lately?"

The other three goons laughed.

"This is all I have," Nathan answered. "I promise you."

"Check the rooms," said Barak. "Be sure to collect a visiting tax from the guests."

"Wait! I do have a few silver coins," Nathan said, hoping this would deter them from inspecting the rest of the inn.

"I thought you might. I know you don't let people stay here for free. You're as greedy as us. But why didn't you say that in the first place? It may have saved you a beating. Probably not, but maybe. "So where are these silver coins?"

Nathan sighed and pointed to a jar near the hearth.

Barak motioned to one of his men to check it out.

"Inspect the rooms," he reiterated to the other two. Nathan nervously listened for any commotion coming from the back room.

Each guest paid their unwarranted tax.

Kezia and the boy refused to breathe when they heard the man enter the room. He looked around briefly but saw nothing save a couple of cushions, two sleeping mats, and the small table. But he did notice a fragrance in the air. It smelled something like cinnamon. The man returned to the front room, where Nathan was still pinned to the ground and bleeding from his nose. One of the other tax collectors was rummaging through the jar Nathan reluctantly told them about.

"Don't take it all," said Nathan. "You already have more than my required tax payment."

Barak grabbed a fistful of Nathan's hair again and whispered in his ear, "Now I know Zacchaeus paid you back four times what we took during our last visit. I don't know if you happened to notice, but Zacchaeus no longer works with us. I'm in charge now, and I'm here to recoup that amount and then some…for my trouble, you see. Do you understand?"

"I don't know what you're talking about," said Nathan. This was not true. Nathan knew exactly what he was talking about. Zacchaeus was a tax collector with a nasty attitude that was much bigger than his stature. He used to be Barak's boss. But Zacchaeus came to the inn alone one recent morning and mysteriously paid Nathan four times what he had taken from him a few months earlier. He said something about an encounter with the prophet who changed his life.

Asher, the man who inspected the back room, reported what he found.

"The last room is empty," he told Barak. "Just a couple of sleeping mats, and it smells of perfume."

"Interesting," Barak said. "An empty room at this time of year? Sounds like you had a good time." He chuckled at his own remark.

"A woman was staying here," said Nathan. "She left yesterday. I'm sure I'll have another guest by the end of the day. You have your money, now go. Don't you have other people to harass?"

Barak grunted and said, "You're my favorite, Nathan."

The other man came back with payments from the guests.

"I'm not convinced you're telling me the truth," Barak said, while counting all the coins. "You're lucky your guests were able to pay their tax. You should thank them. I won't have to squeeze you any harder today. Don't worry. I left you with a few shekels. What can I say? I'm feeling generous."

Barak let go of Nathan and left the inn. Asher and the others stepped on him on their way out. Almost immediately, Nathan could hear his nearby neighbors fighting with them.

He waited a moment to catch his breath. Some of the guests began to come out when they realized the abuse had ended. One of the women staying there gave Nathan a rag to nurse his bloodied nose. He took it and stood to his feet, muttering, "They may as well have been born Roman. And during such a sacred time. They have no fear of God in them." Nathan thanked the woman for the rag and hobbled to the back room. He lifted the table trapdoor. Kezia and the boy climbed out of the hole.

"Look at you," Kezia said. "Our own people abusing us once again."

The boy gently placed his hand on Nathan's shoulder.

"I should no longer hide," the boy said. "I'm old enough to fight."

Nathan smiled and said, "Your mother will kill us both if I let you."

Later that morning, Nathan decided to do whatever it took to make his dream a reality. He had to secure his future. He knew he couldn't do it alone and was thankful for the boy and his mother. But the dream was much too large for the three of them to accomplish on their own. Nathan used the abuses of the rogue tax collectors to his advantage. He went door to door, urging his fellow poor neighbors to help him start a communal vineyard. But many of them were dejected and had already accepted their lot in life. They did not share Nathan's ambition. He also did not command the respect he so desperately needed to accomplish this dream.

"Grow your own vineyard," they'd tell him.

"I don't have enough land for more than a small one," he'd answer. "We'll be stronger if we band together in every way."

The neighbors were not convinced. They also did not approve of the company Nathan kept. Even in that part of town, they despised him for it. He never publicly announced what Kezia did for a living, but everyone noticed she never left. They knew she wasn't his wife, nor the boy his son. They were suspicious of the men who would frequent the inn for only a couple of hours. There was much gossip about what went on in Nathan's inn. Most of it was true.

For several years, Kezia provided a steady stream of income for Nathan, so he agreed to let her stay. She and the boy became like family to him. Kezia was born beautiful. Her hair was dark, thick, and often braided. She wore a bracelet adorned with gemstones, which a man once gave to her as payment for her services. Her bright blue eyes sparkled like diamonds. She left an aroma of cinnamon everywhere she went. Though he imagined it often, Nathan and Kezia were never intimate. Despite his longing, he did his best to raise her son as his own in the absence of his father.

In the afternoon, Nathan began clearing some of the ground and employed the boy's help. Perhaps a tiny vineyard will do for now, he thought. Maybe it will inspire my neighbors to join me sometime.

"Dod?" called the boy, full well knowing Nathan was not his uncle.

Nathan stopped working momentarily to give him his attention. The boy had Kezia's blue diamond eyes. A mirror image.

"Will you marry Mother one day?"

"We need to work a bit faster," said Nathan, ignoring the question and getting back to work immediately.

"I think that would be good," the boy went on. "We're practically a family."

Nathan sighed and said, "We're not a family. And I'm quite certain your father would not approve. Now pick these stones up. Get moving."

"Is there no one else to help us?" the boy asked, as he placed the stones in a wheeled cart.

"Not yet," Nathan answered. "Just us at the moment. Don't be lazy."

"Why do you want a vineyard, anyway?"

"Don't you want a better life for yourself and your mother? I know I do."

"The more money you make, the more they will take. Isn't that true?"

This thought already crossed Nathan's mind. He didn't have it all worked out yet but knew the situation could not continue as it was.

"The rich are not harassed. Only the poor. It will be harder for them to abuse us if we stand together as a community," Nathan said.

"But the community does not want to stand with you."

"That's because they can't see it yet."

"I thought it was because they don't like you."

Nathan said, "Everything will change. You'll see. Are you excited to see your father? I expect he'll be here soon."

Kezia came out and watched them from underneath the shade of the fig tree in front of the inn.

"Mother, I've found some!" her son shouted. He ran over and gave Kezia a bunch of red windflowers.

"Ah, my favorite," she said. "Do you know why God made all the flowers on the third day of creation?"

"Why?" the boy asked, though he heard the answer a thousand times before.

"My mother told me when I was a little girl, it's to remind us that goodness stirs beneath it all, no matter how barren a land may appear. Dead things get buried in the ground and are seemingly lost forever. But soon new growth emerges from the dark earth. Life always finds a way to conquer death."

Kezia smiled at her son's simple gift and placed one of the red windflowers in her hair.

Training

Pontius Pilate left Caesarea with nearly a thousand soldiers. They were going to Jerusalem for Passover to monitor the inflated crowds in the area and ensure no riots broke out. Pilate resented these trips. He had to make a few every year for various religious festivals.

"Fanatics will be the death of me," he mused to his wife, as they set out.

The journey took just under four days. On the first day, the soldiers marched approximately twenty miles and made camp for the night.

In Pilate's army, there was an accomplished centurion named Longinus. He terrified most of his subordinates. Entire cohorts of soldiers parted like the Red Sea when they saw him coming. Not only for his rank and sheer stature but also for his reputation. Only those Longinus trained one-on-one lost their fear of him, for they were permitted to see his humanity and humor. Longinus was promoted after only five years of service for his bravery in several battles and skirmishes. He was known for counting aloud his every kill. He'd look an unfortunate soul in the eyes and say something sharp before bringing his life to an abrupt end.

On one occasion, he slaughtered twin brothers who unwisely attacked him at once. He killed them in such a way as to stack them on top of one another with his gladius piercing through both of them like meat on a skewer. Longinus didn't realize they were related at the time, as they were unidentical, but he nonetheless hated the nickname it had earned him. Soldiers called him *The*

Brother Stacker behind his back but never to his face. Longinus had younger brothers and could only imagine how crushed his mother would be if they all died at once. It was the only kill he felt a shred of remorse about.

In another battle, he killed ten men in ten seconds. The timing can't be validated, of course, but the death count is certain. Most of these battles were revolts and only a handful of sieges. The majority of his service was spent training men, bragging, trash-talking, and drinking—lots of drinking.

He was very much impressed with his new protégé, a young decurion named Marcus, who was recently transferred with a unit from Rome. Not unskilled by any stretch of the imagination, still Marcus improved by leaps and bounds in his swordsmanship over the past few months.

Longinus wanted to get one good training session in before the sun dipped below the horizon. Marcus put his wine down. Longinus did not. The centurion feinted an attack that did not faze his student in the slightest. Marcus countered with a thrust that Longinus parried effortlessly while sipping his wine.

"You'll have to excuse me," he said. "I thirst."

Marcus swung around to hit his mentor's legs. Longinus blocked it but lost his balance in the process and fell. The wine spilled out.

"Now I'm angry," said Longinus. He sprung back up and kicked the gutsy officer square in the chest.

"I'm up to ninety-eight kills, you know?"

Marcus caught his breath as quickly as possible and staggered to his feet. He was no match for the size and power of his superior.

"Really?" Marcus said with a cough. "Ninety-eight, you say? That's impressive."

"Only rarely have I killed someone who didn't deserve it. Who knows, Marcus? You can be ninety-nine. I'll miss you terribly."

"Not likely." Marcus resumed the fight and swung his sword toward Longinus, hitting air only.

"Not bad at all," Longinus said. "If I didn't know any better, I'd say you were *almost* as good as me. I shall rename you…*The Wind Catcher.*"

"Almost as good," Marcus muttered. "I had you on the ground two seconds ago."

"In a real battle," Longinus said, "my dagger would've stabbed your leg at this point. You would've fallen, probably crying like the little baby you are. I would've stood to my feet and thrust my sword into you, saying something clever like, 'Game over.'"

"In a real battle," Marcus rebutted, "I would've ignored the leg pain and thrust my sword into *you* before standing up could even enter your mind. You're lucky this is only a game."

"You apparently have never been stabbed in the leg before." Longinus pointed to his enormous calf scar.

"And yet, you live to tell the tale," Marcus joked.

The two Romans stopped sparring to tend to their drinks. Longinus gulped his wine as fast as he poured it.

"So ninety-eight kills," Marcus mused. "Are you trying to get up to an even hundred?"

"That's when I retire," Longinus said.

"Retire? Would Pilate even let you? You haven't served long enough. What has it been, ten years?"

"A little more. I'll worry about Pilate when the time comes."

"I've only killed maybe twenty or so men," said Marcus, "and have no aspirations to get up to a hundred."

"Marcus, I've recently devoted my life to telling generals-in-training, like yourself, they can only ever aspire to be...*almost* as good as me. Don't feel bad about it. You're good enough to command a squadron of thirty or so. But no more. How many men are in your charge again?"

"Thirty."

"Ah, so you're right where you belong."

"For now," Marcus said. "But you watch and see. And who knows, if you keep up the good work, maybe *I'll* promote *you* one day."

"Marcus, if that were to happen, my father would rise from the dead to smack me."

"It's settled then. I will devote the rest of my life to try and make that happen."

"To the rising of the dead," Longinus said and raised his cup of wine.

"To the rising of the dead." Marcus raised his cup to complete the toast. "Oh!" he added, "and to your dead father smacking you."

The two Romans laughed and drank some more.

Two Roman Friends

Past his bedtime and a bit drunk now, Marcus returned to his tent. Felix, his childhood best friend, was waiting for him outside the tent's entrance. He was a fellow decurion who was also transferred with Marcus from Rome,

"Felix!" Marcus blurted out with slurred speech. "How lovely to see you this fine spring evening."

"I hope you know Longinus has no interest in furthering your career," Felix said. "You're wasting your time. Silvanus on the other hand. Now there's a centurion worth following. Longinus is no match for him. And you are certainly no match for me."

"You want to go right now?" Marcus asked. "You're about as big as Longinus. I'll show you my time has not been wasted." Marcus drew his sword and fell face-forward to the ground. "Hang on, let me get up first."

Felix laughed and offered his hand to pull Marcus up.

"I don't think this will be much of a fight, old friend. There is still a morsel of honor left in my soul."

"I don't believe it," Marcus said.

"Have we not been ordered to stay vigilant in the night hours and always sober-minded, never to be surprised by an attack?"

"What's your point?" Marcus asked. "Are you going to tell on me? Sabotage my promotion?"

"Oh, Marcus. You've already been promoted to decurion. Be content with that. Trust me, you're chasing an impossible dream. An unlikely one at best. You have a lot of competition. Come and sit with me. Have a drink."

"I can really use one," Marcus said.

The two friends sat on a large stone outside their neighboring tents to drink and talk.

"Marcus," Felix began. "Do you ever wonder what it would be like if we Romans were not in charge? Do you think we'd be better off?"

Marcus cocked his head sideways and tried to determine whether or not Felix was serious or not.

"Well," said Marcus, "considering we're Romans...no. Things would not be better for us. What a strange question."

"All kingdoms come to an end," Felix said. "Do they not?"

"I suppose."

"Maybe it's time we..."

Marcus rushed his hand to cover Felix's mouth and looked around.

"Don't finish that sentence," he said. "Have you lost your mind? It's alright to have those thoughts. We all do. But keep them in your head and far away from your mouth."

"This is exactly what I'm talking about?" said Felix. " Do they treat us well, Marcus?"

"Do I have to cover your mouth again? Lower your voice, at least. Our men will hear you." Marcus immediately lowered his own voice to a forceful whisper. "We're high-ranking officers, Felix. We get paid much more than the soldiers under us, don't we? Soon I'll be promoted to centurion and be paid even more. What is there to complain about?"

"Has Judea been any different than Rome for us? Have our conditions changed at all? They tell us what to do. They tell us what not to do. If we don't do exactly what they say, we pay for it. They can only rule with the ever-present threat of violence."

"*They*?" Marcus said. "Don't you mean *we*? Do we not rule our men the same way our superiors rule us? Besides, is there any other way?"

"Peace," Felix said. "We can opt out of this whole thing and let peace govern us."

"So you have lost your mind. In what world does peace accomplish anything? As far as I'm concerned, peace is when your opponent has neither the strength nor the will to fight."

Felix smiled and stood to his feet.

"You must be terrified of freedom," he said.

"I'm not scared of freedom, my friend. I'm scared of being torn asunder, crucified, stoned to death, or forced to fight wild animals."

"Sometimes," said Felix, "those very things are the price of freedom…as well as peace. I'll see you in the morning." And with that, Felix went to his tent for the night.

Marcus stood there in his drunken stupor, trying to process the words of his friend, and wondered if he really had gone mad. He looked up at the stars and the moon for a moment before retiring to his tent, where eight of his men were already fast asleep.

A Dream

Longinus had a dream that night. It was the same one as the night before and the night before that. It was a recurring dream he'd been having for years. He was back in Syracuse. He and his son had just dragged their boat to shore. Kezia was waiting, ready to cook the day's catch. They ate around a fire. There was laughing. They took turns telling stories and singing songs. His mother and siblings were there, along with their families. Soon everyone left for their nearby homes and his son went to sleep. Cherishing this moment alone, he wrapped Kezia in his arms. She looked up from his chest. Her eyes cast a spell on him. He breathed in Kezia's sweet cinnamon scent and kissed her. This dream filled Longinus with hope and delight in the lonely midnight hours. He woke up and whispered to himself, "Three more days." In the meantime, his work provided enough distraction for his aching heart.

The Wealthy Spice Merchant

The visitors had already begun pouring in from the surrounding regions for the past couple of weeks. Some even much earlier than that. One such visitor was named Simon.

Simon arrived in Jerusalem with his wife and three children three months before Passover. He was quite wealthy and his equally rich brother, Caleb, lived there. They built their vast fortune in the spice trade. Because of Simon's excessive wealth, he could travel at will and stay for extended lengths of time whenever and wherever he pleased.

Caleb lived in the Upper City, not far from the high priest. It was an area full of other successful merchants and high-ranking officials. It was the highest point of Jerusalem and so all the elites who lived there were able to look down on everyone else, both literally and figuratively.

Caleb's palace was almost as extravagant as Simon's and only slightly smaller. It was made of stone and marble and had a terracotta roof. The bright mosaic flooring of the reception room had a detailed pattern depicting Moses leading the Israelites out of Egypt. There were several rooms for guests, a large courtyard with a garden, and two private guards who lived on the property in a home detached from the palace.

Simon had always been so proud of their achievements. He and his brother transformed their spice business into an empire. However, his pride fled from his heart the day he met Jesus of Nazareth shortly after his arrival that year. Simon had become rather obsessed with this particular encounter. It was all he could talk about. Months had passed, and yet Simon was stuck. Jesus ruined him.

"How could he say such a thing?" Simon said to his wife, as she desperately tried to sleep.

"I told you a thousand times," Dinah answered. "He was probably crazy. He said one thing to you, and that's all you've been able to talk about since we've been here. How long will you make me suffer?"

Simon ignored his wife's protests and continued.

"Sell all of my possessions and give the proceeds to the poor? *All* of the proceeds? What good would that do? Then we would be poor ourselves! It makes no sense. Then he told me to follow him. Follow him to where?"

"Like I said…crazy."

"But Dinah, I don't think he was crazy. People speak of miracles he's performed. The blind see, the lame walk, one man reportedly rose from the dead."

"Did you happen to see any of those things?" Dinah asked.

"Well, no," replied Simon.

"So what is the problem? They're probably lies. Forget him already."

"I wish I could. But I'm not sure anyone who meets him can forget him. I don't think it's possible. He is a prophet at the very least. Should I ignore the words of a genuine prophet and bring curses upon my family?"

"My dear Simon, choosing to become poor vagabonds who foolishly follow a man we know very little about already sounds like a curse to me. Think of the children. They're your legacy. What would become of them if we lost everything? The twins would become thieves, no doubt. They're already quite mischievous. I don't even want to imagine what our little Joanna would become!"

Simon sighed and said, "I can't help but wonder if that Jesus is exactly right. Maybe what I've been calling a blessing all these years truly is keeping me from the Lord."

"How could you say such a thing? You're the most upright and honest man I know. I'm not saying that because you're my husband. I truly believe it. You've kept all the commandments since your youth! You are a model Jew and a trustworthy merchant. I believe you are blessed for those very reasons."

"That's what *I* told him," said Simon. "And then he told me the one thing I lack."

"Oh, I've heard this too many times. I don't want to hear it again. *You used to have possessions, now your possessions have you.*"

"Exactly right!"

"With that logic why would anyone ever strive to be rich?"

"That's just it, Dinah! He wasn't talking to *all* rich people. He was talking to me. It was like he could see past my heart and soul. And right there, sitting high on a throne—at the center of my life—was wealth and possessions. Somehow he knew that."

Dinah drifted off to sleep in the middle of her husband's rant. This had been going on for several weeks. She could not convince him to forget about his encounter with Jesus. Nor was there anything Simon could do to overthrow the true ruler of his heart.

The night was quiet and the stars were bright. Outside of Caleb's home was an enormous olive tree with thick branches sprawling in different directions and hanging over the property's wall into the front courtyard. Perched deep inside the tree and well-hidden by branches, leaves, and shadows were two thieves named Ehud and Micah.

Two Thieves in a Tree

Caleb admired the enormous tree's beauty and despite its proximity to his wall never saw it as a security problem. This elite area of Jerusalem's Upper City was walled and guarded. And so Caleb lived within walled property within a walled area of a walled city. Furthermore, his two live-in doorkeepers were skilled fighters and master swordsmen. Anyone foolish enough to breach the Upper City and then his property's wall would have to go through one or both of these men before they reached him and his family.

The two thieves hiding in the tree had been studying the routines of Caleb's palace for weeks. When does the family go to sleep? How many people reside there? When do the guards change shifts? Where does the off-duty guard go when his work is finished? They also learned when the caravans and workers come and go to pick up and drop off money, spices, and supplies.

"Surely there is much silver and gold in the house," whispered Ehud. "More than we can carry away on two horses." It was a question they assumed the answer to, but didn't know for sure. They noticed pick-ups and drop-offs were done several days of the week at varying times. But whether or not the money stayed in Caleb's palace or was moved elsewhere remained a mystery.

Micah grunted in agreement and said, "Why else would they have two doorkeepers? I'm sure there's more than enough inside for my mother to live worry-free for the rest of her life."

"Why are you always talking about your mother?" Ehud asked. "You're a real baby, you know that? Don't you have any dreams for yourself?"

"Of course I do. But it wouldn't be right to not take care of my mother, would it? Your mother has been dead for years, so you don't understand."

"I don't understand how a grown man can act like such a baby and be so attached to his mother. Does she still give you milk from her breast?"

"You're lucky we're in a tree right now."

Ehud quietly laughed.

"The real question," Micah said, "is where do they keep all this silver and gold?"

"We'll have to take out both doorkeepers to find out," Ehud noted.

"And from that point, I have my ways of getting information," Micah added. "They've always proved effective. That big fellow is the man who trained me to guard the Upper City walls. Don't like him very much. He was horrible to me. But thanks to him, my arrow can hit any target."

"Do you think while he was training you he had any idea *he'd* be the target one day?" Ehud asked. The two thieves chuckled.

"Shh! He'll hear us," Micah whispered. "Save the jokes for later. We don't make a move until the rebellion starts. That'll make enough commotion for an easier getaway. They should be changing shifts around that time."

Ehud agreed and said, "We'll do our part to support the movement but no more. We have needs of our own. Speaking of which, Barabbas is waiting. Probably already annoyed. We should go now."

As quiet as shadows, the two thieves climbed down from the olive tree.

The Speech

Three miles outside of Jerusalem, Ehud and Micah ran through a patch of woods that led to an open field. They looked at one another in astonishment when they saw the crowd of men gathered. They knew their numbers had swelled, but this was the first opportunity to see them all in one location. There were at least five hundred men present. The property belonged to one of the wealthier Zealots at the gathering.

Ehud and Micah did their best to discreetly slip through the back of the crowd and maneuver their way forward. Everyone waited for Barabbas to speak. The fire crackled in the darkness. It was enough light to guide the two thieves to the front where Barabbas was growing impatient. Ehud and Micah found their places. Barabbas gave them a stern look of rebuke for their tardiness and began the meeting.

"Welcome, men...husbands and fathers...shepherds and farmers...merchants and fishermen...carpenters and masons...My fellow warriors and defenders of the Holy City. We may have our differences." Barabbas stared into the crowd of old and young men, trying to make eye contact with as many members of the group as possible. "We may not see eye to eye on all matters of the law. We don't all have the same wealth. Some of us are more reputable than others. But today, we cast aside those differences and unite under a common cause. We are bound by both blood and purpose. A holy purpose, commissioned by the Lord himself." Barabbas was a carpenter by trade but also a skilled orator by this point in his life. He had given quite a few of these speeches and already led two previous unsuccessful revolts against the Romans in Jerusalem. But his steadfastness and strength of will inspired many Jews who were equally exhausted and frustrated by Roman occupation. The people longed to be an independent kingdom.

"Every one of us is prepared to kill and be killed to free our people and take back our land from gentiles and pagans, those wicked Romans who presume to rule over us. But the Lord is our only ruler. We have no king but God."

The crowd cheered at this.

"The time for us to reclaim our independence is only three days away. People call us the Sicarii, and rightfully so. For we do not wait for our redemption. We take it by dagger and sword. Nor do we expect someone to come and rescue us, for we rescue ourselves."

The crowd cheered again.

"My scouts report a thousand Roman soldiers march with Pontius Pilate."

Men grumbled and growled at the mere mention of the governor's name. Some whispered their anxious thoughts to one another at the idea of so many extra soldiers added to the troops already stationed there.

"The timing is perfect. We are mere days away from our most holy and sacred festival. Pilate comes not to worship, but to monitor. He comes not to keep the peace, but to control us. How many more offenses do we need from this man before we root him out once and for all? Pilate raises golden shields in our holy city bearing Caesar's image. He steals money from the temple treasury to pay for his building projects. He cowardly disguises his soldiers as commoners to club us when we least expect it. He tramples our people with horses. He blasphemes our God until Tiberius rebukes him. Is there no end to his provocation?"

Barabbas stared into the attentive crowd as if expecting an answer to his rhetorical question.

"Well, he has succeeded. We are provoked. But unlike last time, Pilate won't have to wait for Tiberius's rebuke. We will do it ourselves. I hereby sentence Pontius Pilate to death, along with all his cohorts!"

The crowd exploded in applause.

"Yes!" Barabbas shouted. "This is cause for celebration. We are on the cusp of freedom!" He triumphantly raised both fists in the air, then waited for the cheers to die before continuing his speech.

"I want to take some time to address Herod. I don't call him king, for again, we have no king but God. But do not think he's any better than Pilate. Herod only pretends to be our friend. But he who is not our friend is our enemy. Herod even claims to be one of us. He thinks of himself as a devoted Jew."

There were a few dispersed chuckles in the crowd.

"This is a man who married his sister-in-law and comes from a family who murders their own to keep positions of power. What god-fearing Jews would do such a thing? Do not think the fruit falls far from the tree. As soon as we finish with Pilate, we will uproot Herod from his palace as well."

Before continuing, Barabbas provided a moment of silence to let the reality of their mission sink in. He looked at several members of the crowd, then went on.

"At this time, some of you may be tempted to leave. I understand. Perhaps you're frightened. You think of the Roman army as impenetrable. Unbeatable. And so your heart falters. But I should remind you the Lord is our stronghold, whom shall we fear?

"Did not Gideon defeat the Midianite army of more than a hundred thousand with only three hundred men? How was this possible? God gave him the victory.

"Did not David kill the mighty Goliath when he was still a boy? How was this possible? God gave him the victory.

"Did not Judah, son of Mattathias, liberate our city? Did he not cleanse the defiled temple from pagan altars? Did he not drive out an enemy, not unlike our enemy today? How was this possible? God gave him the victory.

"Though we are few, we are mighty. So take heart! Have faith and be encouraged! Lift your eyes to the Lord and let us be the next story of his victory. The new candles of God to light up the darkness."

Barabbas ended his speech by casting a vision of enjoying future Passovers in a free Jerusalem. A new kingdom where the only Romans left would be their subjects, not their oppressors. The crowd of men dispersed into the night. Barabbas, Ehud, and Micah were left alone by the fire.

"How do you think it went?" Barabbas asked.

"Very inspiring," Ehud said.

"I was moved to tears, myself," Micah added.

"This is no time for jokes," Barabbas rebuked. "We may very well be remembered as the small band of brothers to root out an entire empire from our land."

"Or we'll be forgotten as men who tried and were slaughtered," Ehud said.

"Where is your faith?" Barabbas asked, annoyed at both friends. "Without faith, nothing will be accomplished."

"Barabbas," Micah interjected, "is it truly the best time to do this?"

"I'll answer that with a question of my own," said Barabbas. "Is it the Lord's will that his people be ruled by an evil empire forever?"

"Perhaps we should then wait for the Lord to deliver us," said Micah.

"How else does deliverance take place if not by men of God taking a stand?"

Ehud began to laugh.

"And what are *you* laughing at?" Barabbas asked.

"Men of God," Ehud said, still laughing. "Is that what you think we are?"

"Anyone willing to lay down his life to free God's people is a man of God. Is this not true?" This wasn't a rhetorical question. Barabbas wanted his friends to answer.

"I'd rather take someone else's life than give up my own," Ehud said. "We'll be taking many lives if we succeed. Is *this* a godly thing, lest we forget the sixth commandment?"

"There is no other way," Barabbas said. "Evil needs to be dealt with ever so severely. The Lord is about to use us as his instruments of wrath. Surely you're familiar with the Battle of Jericho when our forefathers marched around the wall for seven days, then blew the shofar."

"The walls came tumbling down," said Ehud.

"Exactly!" Barabbas said. "Then they stormed the city and killed their enemy...God's enemy."

"That was different," Micah said. "They had the ark of the covenant back then. The power of God was right there with them."

"Don't you get it?" Barabbas asked. "The power of God lies not in a box, but in our hearts."

"Then I pray the power of God is on our side," Micah said.

"No need to waste your prayers on obvious truths," said Barabbas. "The power of God will be with us. Even more so if that Jesus of Nazareth joins our cause. I haven't met him myself. But I hear stories about him. Hard-to-believe stories. Even if only half of them are true, then God is surely with this man. He certainly has the attention of a great multitude of people. Some of his followers used to be with us. Perhaps we'll persuade him and his men to join our cause."

"He shouldn't be too hard to find," Micah said. "We could use a miracle in our favor."

"Listen to you two," Ehud mocked. "Miracles and magic. Is that what it's going to take? Jesus is a man like us. Nothing more. Nothing less. If we can die, so can he. I say unless he's skilled with a sword, forget about him."

"Maybe you're right," said Barabbas. "All this talk of doubt does make me anxious, though. I need to know you are truly with me. All the way. Let's go over the plan again."

"Again?" Ehud protested. "Are we forgetful fools?"

"Once I give the signal," Barabbas went on, "you two are to start the fire that will spark the revolution. Consider it a burnt offering."

The two chuckled.

"Good one," Ehud said.

"Pay attention." Barabbas was growing impatient with Ehud. "Once the fire has been started, you are to join the fight. Both of you by my side the whole way. We will be a force of three, acting as one. We'll storm the barracks and make our way up to Pilate, himself. I've assigned several men to make sure he doesn't escape. Our entire mission will be foiled if you fail. Do I have your word you will do your part?"

Ehud nodded and said, "You have my word, Barabbas."

"And mine," said Micah.

Barabbas stared at them for a moment, sizing them up. They had known each other for years. But he knew weariness when he saw it. Nevertheless, he smiled and said, "Freedom is coming, my friends. Just three more days."

They left the fire and parted ways. Barabbas went home to his wife and children. Ehud and Micah walked together, as neither had a wife to go home to.

"Are we doing the right thing?" Micah asked.

Ehud laughed and said. "Of course not. We're thieves. Barabbas is a dreamer. If he doesn't want to wake up to the truth, let him sleep. As for me, I am wide awake. We'll start the fire. But we won't stay to fight. We'll make our move on the spice merchant and then disappear."

"But maybe we'll succeed," Micah said. "Maybe we should stay and support Barabbas. Fight till the end. Did you see how large we've grown?"

"I saw," Ehud answered. "And yet, we are no match for the Roman army."

"But if God is on our side—"

"Why would God be on our side? When has God ever supported the endeavors of bandits and thieves?"

"We're also watchmen, sworn to protect—"

"Even richer bandits and thieves?" interrupted Ehud.

"We are only bandits and thieves because of our lot in life," Micah said. "If we were a free people, though?"

"What would change, Micah? We are who we are. That's all we'll ever be. The only thing we need to watch is the spice merchant's money. We've used our position to steal for years now. I'm hoping this will be big enough to retire from all that."

Micah had no response to this. They walked quietly in the night till they reached their ramshackle homes in the Lower City of Jerusalem.

How to Throw a Dagger

Pilate and his soldiers marched for the second day and made camp. Longinus looked forward to his training session with Marcus that evening.

"You know, my first kill was with a dagger, not a sword," Longinus told his protégé.

"Do tell," said Marcus.

"I was seventeen. A beggar came to our door to ask for bread. When my mother refused, for we were poor ourselves, the man pulled out a short sword from under his cloak and threatened to take her life. My mother screamed. I heard her shrill cry while I was with the love of my youth in a nearby forest. I left the girl by a tree and ran as fast as I could. I didn't trust I'd get there in time when I saw her struggling with the man. So I took out my dagger and threw it from where I was, about ten steps away or so. The man stopped what he was doing and dropped his sword. He slowly reached his hand back to feel the dagger sticking out from the base of his neck. Before he could pull the blade out, I did it for him and finished the job. My mother screamed at the carnage happening at the front door of our home. I cleaned the blood off my dagger and smiled at my mother. She slapped me across the face harder than anyone ever has before or since. She said, 'You might've killed me, throwing a dagger like that. How dare you?' I laughed and said, 'A simple thank you would do.' My father would've been proud, but by that time, he had already left us and went back to his hometown in Cappadocia. My mother always said he had to return to his *real* family."

"You told me your father died," Marcus said.

Longinus paused for a moment and looked at the ground.

"He's gone. Whether he's alive or dead, I don't know. He's been dead to me for many years. Doesn't matter, I suppose. But *he* was a man who could throw a dagger and hit his target from a great distance." The centurion lit up at the memory. "Before he left us, my father would spend hour after hour with me. Training me in the art of throwing daggers, helping to hone and perfect my technique. He took great care to pass that skill down to me. Today, I will pass it down to you. There are lots of situations in battles and skirmishes where knowing how to throw a dagger could very well save a fellow soldier's life ."

Longinus unsheathed his dagger and motioned for Marcus to do the same. They walked to a nearby tree.

"Perfect!" Longinus said, finding a fairly young tree with a thin trunk. "I'll go first. We'll start from ten steps away."

Longinus cut some bark off the tree to create a clear target, then walked back to the throwing spot. He briefly went over several throwing techniques. He taught Marcus how to stand, how to grip the dagger, how to maintain momentum, and apply the appropriate amount of force based on the target's distance. Marcus listened intently.

Longinus squinted, raised his arm, then flung the dagger forward with power and grace. It landed almost directly in the center of the barkless target. He smiled but didn't let his pride show too much. He retrieved it and nodded for Marcus to repeat the action.

Marcus got into position, squinted, raised his arm, and launched his dagger toward the tree. Both Longinus and Marcus were pleasantly surprised, as the blade landed a little right from the target's center.

"Not bad," said Longinus. "Not bad at all. Beginner's luck, maybe?"

Marcus shrugged and said, "My father could throw a dagger too, you know? Didn't spend too much time with me on it. But I used to watch him practice."

"We'll see if any of that watching paid off. Let's back it up another ten steps."

They repeated the same exercise. Longinus still landed his dagger near the target's center, but Marcus missed it altogether.

"Almost," said Marcus.

"Almost hitting your target is the same as not hitting your target. In battle, that can cost you your life. It may get a friend killed. Try again."

Marcus tried three more times and finally hit the center from twenty steps away.

"Good job. Let's make it harder still. You!" Longinus grabbed a soldier walking by, eating an apple. "Stand against this tree and don't move. Give me that apple."

Longinus placed the apple on top of the soldier's head and leaned the fruit upright against the trunk of the tree.

"Excuse me, sir," the soldier protested. "I'm not comfortable with this exercise. I should probably practice my dagger-throwing as well. Shall we find another soldier?"

"Relax," said Longinus. "An anxious soldier is a dead soldier. I know what I'm doing."

"But does *he*?" the soldier asked, nodding to Marcus.

"I guess we'll find out. Now don't move. I'll go first again."

Before another protest could leave the reluctant volunteer's mouth, Longinus threw the dagger. The soldier both felt and heard the thud directly above his head. He thought his heart might jump right out of his chest at that moment.

"Aha!" Longinus shouted and ran up to examine his throw. "Look at that!" The blade pierced right through the apple and split it in half. The soldier let out an uneasy laugh and a sigh of relief. Longinus did his best to arrange the split apple pieces together and rest them on top of the soldier's head again. It was now Marcus's turn.

"I'm not sure this is a good idea," Marcus whispered to Longinus. "Perhaps I'm not ready for live practice."

"You'll never know till you try," said Longinus.

"Trying may kill a man. You said it yourself that almost isn't good enough. What if—"

"Are you telling me you're a coward?"

Marcus sighed and readied himself. He could feel his heart beat faster. He did his best to shake off the nerves. He got focused, raised his arm, and kept it up there a bit longer than normal. Finally, he flung his arm forward and the dagger went flying.

The soldier prayed to every Roman god he could name in a few seconds. He also prayed to some ancestors. But as soon as the blade left the shaky hand of Marcus, the soldier moved and let the dagger land directly where his face would've been. He got up, cursed, and took off running as fast and as far as possible.

Marcus and Longinus fell to the ground laughing.

"You're probably, right Marcus," Longinus said, still laughing. "Perhaps you're not ready for live practice. Let's drink, shall we?"

Marcus began walking toward his squad's tents. Longinus walked with him.

"So tell me," Marcus said. "What would someone like you be doing if you weren't a soldier?"

"Ah, that's an easy one. I'd be a fisherman. I've been once since my youth."

"And did you used to count your catches like you count your kills?"

"No, I can't count that high, Marcus. But I would trade my entire career to be back home fishing with my boy."

"You have a son?"

"You'll meet him when we arrive. He lives with his mother just outside of Jerusalem."

"Why not with you? Marcus asked. "Plenty of soldiers keep their families with them, or at least nearby."

"It's safer this way."

"What's the boy's name?"

"What do you think?"

"I thought you were the one and only. So there is another Longinus in the world. I hope you're training him as hard as you're training me."

"He'll know what he needs to know. But I'd rather he become a merchant than a soldier. Why introduce him to unnecessary bloodshed?"

"Isn't bloodshed necessary at least sometimes?"

"Yes!" interjected a third voice to the conversation. "It most certainly is." It was, of course, Felix.

"Longinus, meet my longtime friend, Felix. Felix, Longinus."

The two sized one another up. They were of equal strength and stature. But Longinus was his superior and he had a way of staring at someone new to remind them of this.

"Sit down and join us," Longinus said. "You drink, don't you?" He motioned for Felix to take a seat at the table outside the tents. Marcus poured him a cup of wine.

Felix knew of Longinus and the stories that made him a legend within the ranks. He resented him a bit for how much Marcus looked up to him.

"So tell me, Felix," Longinus said. "What kind of bloodshed do you deem necessary?"

Felix took a big gulp of wine before answering.

"Violence is sometimes necessary to end violence," he said.

"Agreed," said Longinus.

"Defending your family from bandits, for example," Felix said. "Helping the helpless from an attack. Freeing the oppressed generally involves killing."

Longinus laughed at the last one and said, "Quite a statement from an oppressor. Should the unruly not be ruled? There is a certain order in the world. Some are at the top of that order, others at the bottom. It's been this way forever."

"So it has," Felix said.

Marcus watched the two of them, wondering what turn the conversation would take next.

"Would you sacrifice yourself and have your own blood shed for the oppressed?" Longinus asked this and glared at Felix, seeing how he'd answer.

Felix drank some more wine before speaking. Finally, he said, "Shedding *another's* blood would be preferable."

Longinus stared at him for a moment. Then he laughed. Then Marcus laughed.

"You're bold," Longinus said. "I'll give you that. But I'd be careful if I were you. You wouldn't want—I don't know—a superior to misunderstand your words." He let the warning linger in the air for a moment. "But I don't completely disagree with you, Felix. I'd rather my son never have to shed blood at all. Only if it's necessary."

No one spoke for a few seconds. Marcus was torn between his longtime friendship with Felix and his devotion and admiration for Longinus. He needed to break the silence somehow.

"To the shedding of blood, but only if it's necessary," he abruptly toasted. All three raised their cups to meet in the air.

Another Dream

Longinus fell into a deep sleep that night. His dream started the same as usual. Fishing with his son, bringing the day's catch home for Kezia—the love of his life—to prepare a meal, laughing and story-telling with family and friends. Then the dream took a turn. He leaned in to kiss her and she whispered, "Let me go."

"Never," he told her, almost with an incredulous laugh. He grabbed her more tightly.

"Let me go," said Kezia. "Let all of this go."

Longinus looked around. His home began to shake and crumble. He stood to his feet in a panic. Kezia stood there as well but didn't move.

"We have to get out of here!" Longinus shouted.

"Let me go," Kezia said.

"There's no time for this!" He picked her up, threw her on his shoulders, and ran out of the home.

He stopped only a few feet away.

"My son!" He turned around just in time to see the home collapse before his eyes. Then all the surrounding homes in the village collapsed. The mountains in the distance shook and crumbled into dust. The ocean roared and receded. The stars blackened and the sky disappeared. The ground he stood on gave way. Longinus and Kezia fell through the crack. Blackness enveloped them both. He stared at Kezia as they dropped into nothingness.

"What's happening?" he asked.

"Let me go," she said. Kezia caressed his face as they fell. She smiled and then disappeared. Longinus kept falling. But he fell for so long he eventually couldn't tell if he was moving at all. Then he was sure he was merely suspended in the void. He saw someone emerge from the distance and walk toward him. The walk turned into a run. Longinus found himself getting nervous by the second. The runner got close enough for him to see that it was a boy. He recognized the face at once and yearned to run toward him but could not move at all.

It was his son standing in the blackness.

"Abba," he said. His voice echoed. "I'm scared."

Longinus awoke in his tent in the middle of the night, cold, sweating, and out of breath.

"Not even two more days," he muttered. "Almost there." He rested his head once more but did not fall back to sleep.

Brothers

As usual, Caleb and Simon were up well before the sun.

"Let's take a walk in the garden, shall we?" Caleb told his brother.

There were varying stone pathways in Caleb's garden. They chose one and walked, taking deep breaths of the cool morning air. The sound of trickling water from the fountain in the center could be heard from any place in the garden. Soon the sunlight would reveal the vibrancy of the flowers. For now, the fragrance of lavender, mint, and rosemary filled their nostrils. Caleb picked off a pear from a tree and gave it to his brother. Simon took a bite.

"Almost ripe," he said, then tossed the fruit to the ground.

"We need to talk," Caleb said. "Dinah told my wife you're still obsessing over the encounter you've had with that Jesus-of-Nazareth fellow. Are you going to follow him all the way to a futile rebellion against the Romans? Many are saying that's exactly what he's up to."

"That's not any concern of yours, brother, nor your wife's for that matter," said Simon. "And I think you're wrong about him. I'm not convinced he has any interest in governance one way or the other."

"I'm concerned for the business," Caleb replied. "You can have whatever religious epiphany you want. So long as it doesn't cost *me* anything."

"What's yours is yours; what's mine is mine."

"We're partners, are we not? We're stronger together than either of us apart."

"What are you afraid of, Caleb?"

"You becoming a fanatic!" he answered. "You've always had this obsessive side to you. Remember when we were just boys? I was about twelve or so, you must've been about ten. Father invited Joseph ben Caiaphas over for a meal. This was long before he was appointed High Priest, even before he lived in his enormous palace down the road. I don't recall if Annas's daughter was betrothed to him yet. But I remember he and Father would talk for hours. Do you remember that?"

"Of course."

"And you would sit there on the floor listening. Soaking it all in. You were so intrigued with Caiaphas. His knowledge and dedication to the law. How he carried himself. He was all you could talk about for weeks. You wanted to be just like him. No one could force Father to do anything. No one but you. You forced Father to let you study under him."

"I did no such thing," Simon protested.

"You most certainly did. The only thing that altered your rabbinic path was none other than a certain spice trader of Cyrene...another one of Father's guests."

"Ah, yes, Jason. He was a good man. Taught me all I know about the spice business."

"You poured everything you could into learning about it. The whole family wondered if you had abandoned your faith."

"God forbid," said Simon. "Sometimes the Lord reveals different paths for one person. Do you not think it possible to be a successful merchant as well as a man of God?"

"Not for you," Caleb said. "You can do many things, brother. But it seems you are most successful if focused on one thing at a time. Because that has always been you. No matter what you did, you threw your entire self into it. You never went halfway with anything. Always all or nothing."

"It's my obsessive side that's driven the majority of our success."

"Exactly right! Which means it can drive us to ruin as well."

Simon did not respond to this. He felt powerless to change his nature anyway. But he liked the idea of him being a true worshipper of God. He hated the idea he may very well be a worshipper of money instead. But all the evidence now seemed to point to that very truth. A truth that now tormented him day and night. Even when he wasn't thinking about it, he was thinking about it. The jolt of joy he got every time he received a payment. His mounting anxiety when someone missed one. The way he casually felt like a better person than those with lesser means. How giving the tiniest fraction of his wealth convinced his conscience he did enough to help the poor. The money that gave him so much freedom to travel here and there and buy whatever he wanted whenever he wanted was somehow shackled to a pride that rooted him firmly to the earth. He knew there was nothing he could spiritually aspire to, no higher ground to walk on, as long as he was trapped in his love of money. If only I hadn't met Jesus, he thought.

Simon had known for a long time there was something wrong with his life. But it was a vague unsettling. Now there was clarity and he couldn't escape this new knowledge about himself. None of his family understood.

"You have nothing to worry about," he finally told Caleb. "All is well."

"I know you better than that," Caleb said. "But if something were to happen to your side of the business, I may lose half my wealth."

"Poor brother of mine will have to move to a smaller palace," Simon joked.

"What can I say?" Caleb said with a laugh. "I've grown accustomed to this lifestyle." He motioned with his arms to show all his property and possessions, which the rising sun was now beginning to shine on. Then he pointed his finger directly at his brother and said, "Don't go messing it up for me. For us. Your children. Our family's future. You hear me?"

"Relax. I hear you."

"Good. Now forget about that lunatic once and for all. He probably only wanted you to follow him to get your money. That's what I would do if I were crazy."

"What do you mean?" Simon asked. "You *are* crazy. Born crazy in fact."

Caleb growled and then pretended to attack his brother. The two of them laughed as they play-fought in the garden. Dinah and Caleb's wife, Leah, watched through the window, as they prepared breakfast. They smiled at one another.

"Children trapped in grown men's bodies," Leah said.

"Absolutely," Dinah agreed. "They never change."

Later on, when they were all enjoying a leisurely meal, Simon looked at the sundial in the center of the garden near the fountain.

"It's about the sixth hour of the day already," he said. "Shouldn't at least one of your workers have returned by now?"

"Your ever-watchful eyes," Caleb said. "Always on the money, which is where they should be. Don't ever change. Deliveries can sometimes take time. You've been here for this long already, you come at least twice a year, and yet you still worry someone is stealing from you?"

Simon felt the same twinge of shame he'd been feeling for weeks. But he wasn't given sufficient time to ruminate on his brother's words. Little Joanna came running up at that very moment, crashing into him.

"Joy of my life!" Simon shouted. "Be careful with your father. He's not as young as he used to be. What are you up to today, my love?"

"Ethan is showing me how to wield a sword!"

Joanna was swinging a thin stick around as she said this with the fiercest look she could muster.

"Oh, he is, is he?" Simon gave Ethan a stern gaze of disapproval. Ethan simply smiled and walked over from the other end of the garden.

"I think your daughter wants my job, sir."

Simon leaned in to speak quietly and said, "Didn't I tell you to train my *boys*? I was hoping with all your sword mastery, you or Elijah would pass some of those skills on to them. We've been here for several weeks already and my sons still fight like untrained monkeys."

"I would train your sons, but I never know where they are. Besides, she's having fun. And I don't think my eyes deceive me, sir, but she's not half-bad. I see potential. Great potential."

Joanna then pretended to stab Ethan in the stomach, yelling, "Ahhh!" In great dramatic flair, Ethan dropped to his knees and said, "You got me. But I will never fear you, Joanna. People can only harm the body, but never the soul." Then he fell to the ground face-up, as if dead.

"This is not a game for girls," Simon protested. "Where are your brothers, Joanna?"

Still laughing at Ethan's antics, she said, "I don't know. Running around somewhere."

Ethan stood to his feet and laughed.

"He lives," Joanna said in a make-believe evil voice, raising her stick in a threatening way.

"Have mercy," Ethan said, then took off running out of the garden.

Simon looked at Leah and said, "A bit immature, that guard of yours. Running around with children like a fool."

Leah laughed.

"Oh, stop," she said. "He's only having fun. Caleb and I have no children of our own for him to tease and carry on with."

"Why does he need to tease and carry on with children at all? He's supposed to be a fighter and protector of your home. His personality should be serious. Like that Elijah fellow of yours. Now there's a man to be frightened of. Reminds me of my own guards back home."

"Elijah's his uncle, and he's old and cranky. Ethan still has the spark of life in him, being not more than a youth himself. Let him be. Your daughter thinks of him as family. Tell me, are you afraid your little Joanna will grow up and marry a warrior?"

"No," said Simon. "I'm afraid she will grow up and *become* a warrior."

Ehud and Micah ended their tower shifts abruptly. They were still dressed in uniform as Upper City watchmen. They had seen the caravan enter the gate from the towers they were stationed at. They knew exactly where the band of spice traders were going. They each found a watchman to replace their spot on the towers so they could patrol the area. They got on their horses and followed close behind the caravan.

"I still don't understand why we can't attack them directly before they even reach Caleb's palace," Micah said. "We have swords and daggers, bows and arrows, and more importantly horses to make a quick getaway."

"A quick getaway?" said Ehud. "Do you not see all the people with them? They have the same weapons as us and there's more of them. Not to mention all the Roman soldiers roaming about paid to protect the rich."

"All I'm saying is why should we wait to fight guards behind a gate on private property? Surely all these caravans coming and going travel on secluded roads from time to time. We've been very successful on those roads in the past."

"They purposely stay on the more crowded routes to avoid people like us. They know what they're doing. We have to be smarter than that."

"So it's your way or nothing, in other words. As always."

Exasperated, Ehud turned to his longtime friend and partner in crime and said, "It's my way or certain death, you fool. This may be our biggest score yet, and you want to risk it all. Why steal an apple if you can take the whole tree?"

"What in the world are you talking about?" Micah asked. "I don't want any apples."

"It's just a saying, Micah. Never mind."

The caravan arrived at Caleb's palace. Ehud and Micah strolled past on their horses and looked in when Ethan opened the gate.

"Aha!" Caleb cried out. "Do you smell that?"

"Frankincense?" asked Simon. "Myrrh? Cinnamon?"

"No," Caleb answered. "I'm talking about the smell of success, my dear brother. You can quit your worrying." He nodded to Ehud and Micah when he noticed the Upper City watchmen looking in, grateful he lived in such a protected area of Jerusalem. They nodded back out of feigned respect.

The men in the caravan began to immediately unload their camels, donkeys, mules, and horses. Ehud and Micah noticed many sacks that looked heavy enough to be filled with gold or silver. They smiled at one another slightly, but not enough to break character. Their horses picked up from a walk to a trot, then finally a canter till they were out of sight.

Reason to Fear

It started to rain. Barabbas was pacing about in the leaky shack he called home. His wife Deborah was visibly annoyed, but he was too lost in his thoughts to notice.

"Why are you so anxious?" she asked.
"You know why I'm so anxious," he said.
"Yes, I do."
"Then why do you ask?"
"Is everything ready?" she asked.
"As ready as it can be."
"Have your numbers increased?"
"They have."
"Have the traitors been paid?"
"They've been paid half. They'll get the other half when the job is done. That was the agreement."
"Do you believe God is on your side?"
Barabbas turned to face his wife and said, "Of course I do."
"Then I ask again," she said, "Why are you so anxious?"
Barabbas knew the answer to the question but didn't want to say it. He was scared. Plain and simple. Revolts against the Romans generally didn't end well for the perpetrators. He had been involved in a minor one a couple of years prior and lost one of his best friends. Ehud and Micah took part in that tiny revolt as well. They managed to kill two Roman soldiers before barely escaping with only their lives. Nothing had changed. The Romans still occupied the land. The oppression continued. In a moment of vulnerability, Barabbas decided to share a thought with his wife.

"Do you have any idea what they do to insurrectionists?"

Deborah caressed her husband's face.

"My dear, either freedom is worth the fight or it isn't. Would God have us to be ruled by evil men forever? Has there ever been an empire God hasn't delivered us from? Egyptians, Babylonians, Philistines, Assyrians, Persians, Greeks."

Barabbas nodded along in agreement.

His wife stared into his eyes and said, "It's time to add Romans to that list."

He took a deep breath and felt strengthened to carry on.

"Maybe *you* should lead the revolt," he said.

Deborah laughed and the couple embraced.

"And who knows?" she added. "Maybe all the travelers and visitors will be inspired to join in. That would completely overwhelm the Romans."

Barabbas said nothing to this. He knew Pilate and his army would crush that very scenario from happening.

Tour of the Palace

The journey was met with few complications, save a couple of twisted ankles. The Roman army marched into Jerusalem before dusk on the fourth day. The soldiers on foot were in ranks and files, led by centurions and other high-ranking officials on horseback. Pilate and his wife rode in a carriage. They looked on in irritation at the city buzzing with Passover pilgrims from every direction. Worshippers traveled from the Decapolis, Cyrene, Egypt, and some even as far as Rome. The visiting Jews along with several of the city's residents jeered at Pilate's parade of power.

Many soldiers were sent to the Antonia Fortress near the Temple Mount. Others followed Pontius Pilate to the Praetorium. This was the governor's palace on the Western Hill next to Herod's residence. Pilate entered unmoved—even bored a little—by the crowd's disapproval. After a quick briefing, he and his wife went straight to their private chambers on the upper floor. He ordered a servant to fetch him a bowl of grapes at once.

Longinus and most of the centurions had private rooms. He, Marcus, Felix, and other high-ranking officials were staying at the Praetorium with Pilate. They led their men to the barracks, where they'd reside for the duration of the trip.

"Walk with me, Marcus," said Longinus, after unpacking their belongings and supplies.

The two exited the barracks and walked the hallway above the pit, where prisoners accused of serious crimes were sent to await trial.

"Before the party begins," said Longinus. "I wanted to show you around. You've seen similar facilities back in Rome, so nothing should be too surprising. This is not unlike the palace in Caesarea."

Longinus showed Marcus the armory. He took him to varying administrative offices, the kitchen, the shrine, and the servants' quarters.

As they approached the roofless punishment room, Longinus found it odd he heard whipping and thrashing, but no moans of pain coming from the prisoner on the receiving end. He and Marcus stepped into the courtyard to investigate. Two soldiers were whipping a nearly naked man. They stopped and stood upright when they saw the centurion enter.

"What is this man guilty of?" Longinus asked.

One of the soldiers answered, "Treason. He's one of our own."

All four of them spat on the ground in unison.

"The traitor has been charged with several counts of conspiracy," the soldier added. "He killed at least five of us. He's been sentenced to die."

"How many lashes has he received?"

"Only three from each of us so far."

Longinus asked to see the whip being used to administer the punishment. He examined it and appeared visibly disappointed.

"For such grievous crimes," Longinus said, "there is no need to hold back. He's going to die anyway. Are we sympathizing because he's Roman?"

"Never!" the soldiers said in unison, then spat on the ground again.

"Good," said Longinus. "We should be all the more harsh for this very reason."

The prisoner froze in fear, listening to this conversation. His arms were raised and tied to a tree in the courtyard's center. He began to cry and convulse at the thought of what was about to happen. The whip being used was common for lesser crimes.

"This man can take more pain than average," Longinus said, "and deserves to." He then walked over to the torture devices hanging on a wall. There were several spiked gloves, batons with protruding nails, slingshots, bludgeons, and ropes. In front of the wall were three cauldrons brimming over with scalding wax. Longinus finally settled on two flagrums.

He showed Marcus how pieces of bone, metal, and rock were attached to the leather thongs for efficiency.

"Here," Longinus said to the soldiers. "Try these instead."

Each soldier whipped the prisoner three times. Every lash produced a scream, followed by a whimper. Marcus and Longinus wiped the splashed blood from their faces."

"There," Longinus said. "That's more like it."

They left the soldiers to it and continued with the tour.

"If you're going to be a good centurion, Marcus, you must make sure the punishment fits the crime. Adjust accordingly when it doesn't."

Longinus walked Marcus to the atrium where they first entered.

"We're done for now," he said. "I have some personal matters to attend to. I'll be back by morning. Hopefully sooner."

"You'll miss all the festivities and—more importantly—the wine," said Marcus.

"You'll have to save me some, good man."

"No promises," said the centurion-in-training. "Maybe a cup or two. You are my mentor, after all. It's only right."

"Right would mean a bottle or two, Marcus. A cup or two is for babies. Don't let your greed get you thrown into the pit."

Marcus smiled at his mentor's sense of humor and was grateful such a ferocious soldier had a lighter side. Longinus exited the palace and got on his horse. Marcus went to look for Felix.

Family

The guards at the city gates bowed their heads in respect when they saw the enormous commander pass, who looked even bigger sitting high on the black stallion. Longinus was dead tired and so was the horse. But exhaustion would not stop him from seeing Kezia and his son, who were only two short miles from the city.

When Longinus arrived at the inn, he tied his horse and drew water from the well. Nathan came running out to greet him.

"Nice to see you, Longinus. I thought you might've come earlier."

Longinus embraced the innkeeper whom he had known for several years.

"Good to see you as well, Nathan. How are you? Hopefully better than your face."

"Ah, well, tax collectors again." Nathan motioned to his battered cheek and eye when he said this. He wished he was able to hide them. "Otherwise, I'm fine. Please go inside. I'll take care of your horse. They'll be so excited, I'm sure."

Longinus gave Nathan two denarii for his kindness. Nathan looked at the silver in his palm and thanked him, then went to fetch grain for the horse. Longinus walked inside the inn.

The sun had now set. The guests in the dimly lit common area shuddered when they saw the centurion. He greeted them kindly enough to calm them down. Then he walked to the back room. Kezia and the boy sat on cushions opposite each other, discussing the day's events. Longinus cleared his throat to get their attention.

Kezia panicked and did not recognize who it was at first. She told her son in Aramaic to go outside and help Nathan. Kezia then quickly removed the delicate red windflower from her hair and grabbed a comb from the table, thinking it was a new customer. She stopped when her son said, "Abba!" This always made Longinus feel his boy was more Jewish than Roman. Most of Pilate's men knew enough Aramaic to communicate with the locals. However, Longinus had made a point to become fluent the very day he met Kezia.

She looked up and stared at Longinus through the dark. Their son had already thrown himself into his arms.

"My boy," Longinus said. He squeezed him till he couldn't breathe.

"Don't kill him," said Kezia.

"I'm sorry, son. Couldn't help it. Now I want to hear all about your life and recent adventures. But why don't you first do as you're told and help Nathan outside for a bit while I catch up with your mother."

The boy ran outside with an extra pep in his step.

"He's getting big," Longinus said with a smile. "I'd ask how old he is but I can never forget. I was a brand new soldier when we first met. Right in this very inn."

Longinus grabbed Kezia into his arms. He moved his lips toward hers but she turned her face.

"It's been a while since your last visit," she said. "What took you so long?" Kezia then wriggled out of his powerful arms.

"What, no kiss?" he said. "Pilate keeps us busy. Why are you still doing this?"

"Doing what? I'm not doing anything."

"You know *what*," said Longinus. He fondled her jewelry and took a big whiff of her cinnamon perfume. "Didn't I give you enough money to last till now?"

"It would've been," she said. "But Nathan needed it."

"*His* debt is not *your* debt."

"I live here, don't I? Tax collectors do what tax collectors do. Sometimes he owes other men money...bad men. I do what I can to help."

"Once again, Nathan's problems should not be yours. That money was for you and our son. For food and lodging. Not for Nathan to pay debts he shouldn't owe in the first place. I'll kill him. He won't owe another soul." Longinus grabbed the hilt of his dagger.

"You'll do no such thing," Kezia reprimanded and stopped his hand from unsheathing the blade. "The tax collectors abuse us every chance they get. That's not his fault. Nathan isn't perfect, but he's kind."

"Kind enough to waste my money," Longinus mumbled.

"You gave the money to *me*. Remember?" She turned her back to him to face the small hole in the wall to peek at what Nathan and her son were doing outside. The boy was wielding a stick at Nathan, pretending he was a centurion.

Longinus grabbed Kezia's arm and swung her around to face him.

"I need you to listen to me," he said. "This horrible life you're living ends tonight. You're coming with me. You and Longinus. You're my family."

Kezia laughed incredulously.

"Family?" she said. "Is that what you call this?"

"Yes! I dream of you every night. I know it's crazy, but you're all I have. I love you with everything in me."

Kezia sighed and caressed his face. "This again? Men don't love women like me."

"You're wrong, Kezia."

"Or have you forgotten? That we are not your *real* family. I'm a substitute wife. Someone to make you feel like a whole person from time to time. Your son is no different. He's a temporary substitute."

"This couldn't be further from the truth. Come with me. Tonight. You'll see there's no one else."

"Come with you?"

"To the Palace."

"Where, the barracks? I'll be raped! Are you crazy?"

"No one would dare."

"Longinus, your people don't exactly like my kind. You know that. You must know that."

"It's temporary. For the festival. Plenty of soldiers have wives with them in the barracks. You won't be the only woman."

"Will I be the only *Jewish* woman?"

"Maybe."

"A Jewish prostitute and a Roman centurion together?" she pondered. "Scandalous. And what about our boy? I thought you didn't want him to become a soldier. It's bad enough he's a Roman citizen by birthright. I thought you wanted to keep it a secret. Don't you think it will be all he wants once he gets a taste of staying with the mighty Romans? No, I can't allow it. And what about Nathan?"

"Nathan! He's going to get you both killed, Kezia. Forget Nathan. And don't worry about Longinus."

"How can I not? He bears your name."

"That doesn't mean he has to bear my nature."

"Our gods are different," she added.

"Your god will be my god. I'll forsake all others."

"Just like that? You'll abandon all the gods of your people to be with one woman? Treason! And how will my god know you'll be faithful to *him*?"

"May he strike me dead if I'm not," said Longinus. "Stay with me till Pilate leaves Jerusalem. If you want to return here, I won't keep you against your will. Though I pray that you come with me to Caesarea. My accommodations there are perfect for a family."

"You *pray* that I come with you? And just who is that prayer to?" she asked. "Your god or mine?"

He held her hands and brought them to his lips for a kiss. He stared into her sparkling eyes in the dimly lit room.

"Let me go," she said and pulled away. Kezia stared at Longinus. He came closer and forced his kiss on her. She fought only for a second and then fell into it. Finally, she wrapped her arms around him.

"I don't know," she said. "Are you sure about this?"

"More than anything else," he said.

Kezia was still not convinced, but she knew her life could not go on as it was. She wanted nothing more than for their son to be safe. Surely the boy's father could do a better job than her, she reasoned.

They broke the news to the boy and Nathan. The boy cheered.

Nathan felt a lump form in his throat. It was as though the earth opened up and swallowed him whole. His thoughts were moving faster than the words could form in his mouth. Nathan stuttered when he protested, "Wait a minute. You can't do this to me. I need the income."

"You'll have to find someone else, old friend. Kezia's done with this life. But here's some money to hold you over." Longinus handed Nathan a small pouch of denarii worth a few weeks' wages. "Don't be foolish with it and—for the love of all that is sacred—don't let the collectors know about it!"

"Easy for you to say," replied Nathan. "I'm not exactly a warrior if you hadn't noticed. Am I to lie to the man with his foot on my neck?"

"It matters not where his foot is, so long as he doesn't discover the money. He won't kill you. There would be nothing to collect if he did."

Nathan suddenly thought of a new use for the secret hole in the backroom's floor. He thanked Longinus for his generosity.

"I'll need an extra horse for the night," Longinus said. "You can have it back in the morning."

Nathan reluctantly obliged. Longinus went inside with his son to get the rest of their belongings.

The air was cool and comfortable. Nathan stared at Kezia in disbelief.

"Did you think I'd stay forever?" she asked.

He looked down at the ground and said, "I don't know what I thought. All I know is that whenever I dream about the future. The vineyard. You and the boy are there. What does my future look like now?"

Kezia brought her finger to Nathan's chin and forced him to look up at her.

"Thank you for everything, Nathan. I'll never forget you. I pray the Lord gives you your vineyard."

Nathan wanted to tell her a million things, but he could say nothing. She kissed him on his swollen eye. He wiped his tears away when Longinus and the boy came back out.

They packed the few belongings they owned. The boy gave his mother the red windflower she put in her hair earlier.

"Ah, thank you," she said. "I almost forgot."

Longinus helped his family onto the horse and smiled. He knew he wouldn't dream that night, for his dream had finally come true.

It suddenly dawned on the boy he was leaving the man he spent most of his days with. The one he affectionately called Uncle. The one who had been raising him as his own.

"Dod," he said.

Nathan smiled at the boy and patted his shoulders hard with both hands.

"You know where I'll be if you need me," he said.

Nathan stared at them as they rode away from the inn. Kezia and the boy looked back only once.

"It'll be easier if we don't look back again," she said.

Her mind was in a whirlwind. Kezia began to ruminate on her life's journey. The last time she was in the city, several men tried to kill her. She suddenly became overwhelmed with shame and wondered what her parents would think if they were still alive. Her life as a prostitute, getting mixed up with a Roman man, especially one whom she knew participated in the oppression of her people. It was all too much to dwell on. Her parents were Zealots and hated the Romans more than anyone she knew. They were both killed in an unsuccessful revolt when she was only twelve.

As they approached Jerusalem, Kezia whispered a simple prayer: *Lord, forgive me.* The boy heard it but didn't comment. He was too enthralled with the whole adventure of it all.

The Roman guards opened the city gates as soon as they saw the centurion approach and bowed their heads as he passed. Longinus tied his horse in the stables and found a soldier to return the one that belonged to Nathan.

"That was kind of you," Kezia said. "Returning Nathan's horse so promptly."

"Well, I wish to never see him again. So…problem solved."

They entered the governor's palace. In complete wonderment, the boy stared at the marble columns and high ceilings. Echoes of fun and laughter reverberated around the huge hall. Kezia couldn't tell where the commotion was coming from. There were only guards patrolling the floor and officials conversing. Many of them stopped what they were doing to greet the centurion as he passed. Kezia found it disorienting that most of them spoke Latin to one another in this strange place. She spoke Greek, Hebrew, and Aramaic but never had a reason to learn the devil's language, as her parents often called it. But the respect Longinus commanded made Kezia feel important for once in her life.

Longinus led his family to a set of doors. The sounds of partying only grew louder as they approached, then finally exploded when the doors opened. There were drunken soldiers everywhere, some with women in their arms. Whether or not these women were their wives was not obvious. Even children were running around chasing one another and playing games. There was live music and dancing.

"We like to celebrate after a long journey," Longinus shouted to Kezia, trying to compete with the noise.

"I see that," Kezia shouted back.

The boy was awestruck at everything his eyes were seeing. His mother wanted to cover them for some of it.

They kept walking till they reached another set of doors. The noise continued as they entered the barracks. Though her face was veiled, Kezia noticed all the men staring as she walked by. She kept close to Longinus.

She thought she recognized a few faces but wasn't sure. One drunken soldier blew her a kiss. Longinus unfortunately noticed. He grabbed the soldier by the front of his face and smashed the back of his head into the stone wall behind him. The soldier collapsed to the ground like a lifeless sack. Longinus didn't bother to check whether the soldier survived. Everyone else looked away and minded their business after that.

Longinus's private room was better than Kezia expected. There was even a table of fruit and bread for them. The boy ran to it and began devouring.

"It's like you never feed him," said Longinus.

"He's a growing boy," Kezia replied.

Longinus closed the door and removed Kezia's veil.

"You're safe with me," he said and kissed her. "Eat, have some fruit. I want to show you around. I'll introduce you to the man I'm training if he's not completely drunk by now. Let me go find him. I want him to know what you two look like. You can trust him to keep you safe in my absence."

"You're leaving me in this room?" Kezia said, alarmed at the very notion.

"You can bar the door if you like. When I come back I'll knock like this." Longinus knocked on the wooden fruit table in a pattern of two knocks, followed by a short pause, then three more knocks.

"Relax," he told her. "You'll be much safer here than you ever were with Nathan."

He left the room to go find Marcus. Kezia locked the wooden bar in place. Staring at her boy still eating fruit, she asked him, "So what do you think?"

He smiled and said, "I love it here."

Kezia smiled back but didn't share the sentiment. The soldiers could be heard laughing and shouting through the walls. How she would ever be able to fall asleep, she didn't know. She grabbed an apple from the table and found a chair.

The Spark

Micah wanted to retreat. He could feel his heart in his chest. It beat faster and harder the closer he got to the Praetorium. But there was no turning back. He went into character, as did Ehud. They rode in the back of the Roman traitor's wagon being pulled by two horses. They sat there quietly in the dark, listening to the clip-clop of the horses' hooves. The wagon was full of Roman supplies from the Antonia Fortress. The traitor was none other than Silvanus the centurion. Ehud and Micah were to act as his servants.

Longinus knew Silvanus quite well, but not well enough to know he'd betray his own people. Silvanus was about to retire and return home. Barabbas paid him half his money upfront, as that was the agreement. Even if that was all the Roman received, it was enough to last the centurion for years to come. Barabbas had successfully convinced several rich men to sponsor his efforts against Roman occupation and was now seeing the power of wealth in his movement. Not only this, but Silvanus managed to get Barabbas everything he needed to look like a centurion and thus ensure unquestioned respect from the soldiers. Barabbas was grateful but did not feel at all comfortable in the heavy armor and oversized helmet that kept slipping out of place and blocking his vision. He tried his best not to look awkward as he guarded the entrance to the palace.

Kezia was nodding off to sleep. Her eyes were closing, as she watched her son play *centurion* across the room. She was startled to alertness when she heard the rhythmic knock on the door letting her know it was Longinus. She put her veil back on and removed the wooden bar.

"Kezia," Longinus said, "This is Marcus. I'm training him. He'll make sure no harm overtakes you whenever I'm gone. But please show him your face so he knows what you look like."

Reluctantly, she removed her veil.

"A pleasure to meet you," Marcus said. He was quite drunk. "Your security will be the finest in all Judea."

"And this is my son," Longinus said.

"What's your name, boy?" asked Marcus.

"Longinus," he answered.

"Like your father. How appropriate. And judging by your sword, you must also be a mighty warrior like him."

The boy laughed when he realized he was still holding his stick like a sword.

"Can you throw a dagger like your father?" asked Marcus.

"You can throw a dagger?" the boy asked his father excitedly.

"And hit a target from several steps away!" Marcus added. "Oh, it's settled. We'll have to show you right now. Get an apple from the fruit table, my boy. Then go stand against the wall over there. You're going to put the apple on your head and your father will throw the dagger from here, only hitting the apple, not your head. Watch this. It's amazing. You'll see."

"Absolutely not!" Kezia protested. The two Romans laughed at the suggestion and so did the boy.

"Let me show you around," said Longinus. "You may go now, Marcus. Training in the morning."

Marcus staggered away and clumsily bumped into the walls calling out, "Felix, where in the world are you?"

Kezia and the boy followed Longinus out of the room.

The corridor was dimly lit with oil lamps mounted on brackets along the stone walls. Soldiers were still drinking, laughing, and philandering. Most of the children were sent to bed already. Longinus gave his family a tour of the palace but did not take them to the punishment room. They finally reached the atrium's entrance where they came in.

Barabbas tried not to breathe when the centurion and his family came outside and stood next to him. He kept his eyes straight ahead.

Longinus was surprised to see so many soldiers outside not

doing much of anything. He looked up at the sky.

"I like to come out here and stare at the stars," he said. "I love to breathe in the fresh air." He turned to Barabbas and said, "Why so serious, friend?" Barabbas did not speak Latin and nearly froze to death from fear. He simply smiled and nodded.

"Well, look who it is." Longinus saw the wagon approach. Then he whispered in Kezia's ear, "Silvanus thinks he's better than all of us."

Barabbas did his best to visually count his fighters. Close to four hundred men met earlier that day in the same field he gave his speech. Barabbas was not convinced everyone showed up for the main event. It was impossible to know for sure, as the Zealots were dressed like anything from Roman soldiers to common peasants or travelers.

Silvanus dismounted his horse and greeted Longinus.

"My wife and son," said Longinus, proudly presenting Kezia and the boy.

Silvanus nodded and said, "They should probably go back to your private quarters. The men have been marching for a few days and have already been drinking for hours. Not a place for women and children. I wouldn't want them to get hurt."

"Thank you for your concern, Silvanus. But they're safe with me."

Longinus noticed something in his fellow centurion's eyes he didn't like. He'd seen it countless times, as it takes a killer to know a killer.

"So be it," Silvanus said. He then looked at Ehud and Micah in the back of the wagon and gave them the signal. The two thieves came out. Ehud held two lit torches. Micah held a large container of tar. A wave of relief came over Barabbas when he saw them. The plan was coming to fruition.

Silvanus instructed two guards standing near Longinus to help his "servants." They did as they were told and walked behind the wagon.

"Have a lovely evening," Silvanus said to Longinus and his family. Addressing Kezia and the boy, he added, "Welcome to the palace." He then walked away.

"Abba, who is stronger?" the boy whispered. "You or him?"

"Who do you think?" Longinus responded with a laugh. They turned around to go back inside.

"What do you need help with?" one of the guards asked.

"Silvanus wants you to hold this?" said Micah before quickly splashing both guards with tar. The dumbfounded soldiers went to unsheathe their swords but without a second wasted Ehud used his torches to light them both on fire before they got the chance. Engulfed in flames, they started screaming and running around in a panic. Longinus turned around to see what the commotion was about. He yelled into the Praetorium, "Fire! Fire!"

"We should go back to the room," Kezia said frantically. Longinus did not hear her, being caught up with the situation at hand. She wasn't sure what to do or where to go.

Aside from all the noise from the partying and music, it also took a while for the Romans to snap out of their drunken stupor. However, two soldiers in the building responded to the call. When they reached outside, one of the engulfed soldiers was already dead and on the ground, the fire still burning. The other was desperately searching for water, unable to find any.

"We need water!" one of the soldiers yelled. "Quickly!"

The other responder ran to a nearby well to draw a bucket of water. When he turned around to rush to the soldier's aid he was met with a dagger in his heart by Silvanus. Seeing this entire encounter take place, Longinus drew his gladius.

"We're under attack!" he yelled.

The charred soldier still engulfed in flames gave up hope and fell to the ground dead. The revolt had officially begun.

Barabbas was waiting for Ehud and Micah to come beside him. Instead, he saw them riding off with the centurion's horses. He screamed out of frustration and pulled out the gladius Silvanus equipped him with. The other rebels followed suit, pulling out daggers, swords, and clubs. They all screamed a war cry, then started chanting, "We have no king but God! We have no king but God!" Sword already drawn, Longinus ran toward Silvanus who was waiting for him.

By this time, the Romans inside got word they were under attack and began pouring out of the Praetorium like cockroaches. Kezia tried desperately to get back inside but it was no use. She and the young Longinus were nearly trampled. Marcus ran outside and saw them. He did his best to protect them but finally said, "I have to fight. Hide behind this column. Don't draw any attention to yourselves. I'll come back as soon as I can!" Marcus drew his gladius and ran toward the rebels. Kezia grabbed the boy close to her chest and covered him against the column.

Silvanus was quite larger than Longinus, but nearly twenty years his senior. Still, his strength was unmatched by most in Pilate's cohorts. Longinus felt his power immediately when their swords clashed. He growled like an animal and summoned everything within him to meet the challenge. Steel against steel clanged as the two thrusted, slashed, and blocked one another's maneuvers.

Forget Ehud and Micah, Barabbas thought. I'll have to fight with triple the strength. Barabbas began attacking Romans who were already confused by his centurion disguise. He swiftly killed two. The rest of the rebels followed suit. They had the upper hand at first as it took time for the rest of the Romans to get out of the palace. By the time they did, it was difficult to distinguish soldier from insurrectionist. Herod's soldiers came to help the visiting army. Soon Barabbas and his men were overwhelmed. A wave of fear fell on them. To make matters worse, the Romans were not the only ones confused. Some of the rebels began accidentally killing their own as well.

Barabbas looked on in horror. Seeing the carnage and impossibility of winning, many rebels fled at this point. Then Barabbas noticed Silvanus and Longinus fighting. He was grateful for the traitor's help and wanted to return the favor. He ran toward them intending to stab Longinus in the back to help Silvanus.

In a brief moment of clarity and panic, Kezia opened her eyes to see what was happening. She noticed Barabbas running toward Longinus from behind.

"Your father!" she shouted to her son, still shielding him against the column. "Don't move from here."

Kezia wasn't sure what her plan was. There was no plan. Perhaps she could provide a brief distraction and buy Longinus enough time to handle it himself. No one was fighting near the column, so she felt her boy was safe enough for the time being. She ran toward Barabbas. Barabbas charged at Longinus with his sword pointing forward. Kezia caught up to him, grabbed his shoulder, and shouted with everything in her, "No!"

Instinctively, Barabbas turned around and thrust his sword in and through Kezia. She looked down, as Barabbas pulled out his blood-drenched sword. He was just as shocked as Kezia, realizing he had stabbed a woman and not a Roman soldier. She trembled, coughed up blood, and looked back at her horrified son. She stared at Barabbas and managed to quietly say, "Now go, and sin no more." She closed her eyes and collapsed to the ground.

"I'm...I'm...I'm so sorry," Barabbas stuttered. But there was no time.

Marcus had just finished killing a rebel when he witnessed Kezia's murder. He made eye contact with Barabbas. The Zealot's clunky movements and loose helmet gave away his false identity almost instantly. Barabbas then looked around and saw how his men were getting crushed. The ones with enough strength already fled.

"Mother?" the young Longinus shouted from behind the column.

"Go back to the room, boy!" said Marcus. "Bar the door. I'll come for you when this is over." The shocked boy did as he was told and ran back to his father's private room in the barracks.

Marcus watched Barabbas run to the stables and get on a horse. Their eyes met. Barabbas spat on the ground in protest. He cued the horse to move and the oversized helmet slid over his eyes immediately. He rode blindly for a moment till he managed to adjust it.

"Try to get past the city gates," Marcus said to himself, as Barabbas rode off. "I will find you. I promise you that."

Longinus had yet to learn of Kezia's demise. But he finally beat Silvanus with a final thrust of his gladius into the elder centurion's heart and through his back. He drove the sword with Silvanus stuck to it into the ground and then twisted the blade.

"I hope you were paid well," he said "You're number ninety-nine, my friend." Silvanus coughed up blood and smiled. This confused Longinus a bit. Before he could realize what was happening, Silvanus pulled out the dagger from his belt's sheath and forcefully stabbed Longinus in his left eye as a final attack. Longinus screamed and yanked the blade from his eye. He stood to his feet in rage and pain. Silvanus laughed himself to death.

The eye bled profusely and Longinus did his best to press it with his left hand; he pulled the gladius out of his dead opponent. The revolt was almost finished. Longinus tried to orient himself to see what was going on around him, albeit from one eye. A rebel came screaming at him with his sword raised to the sky. Longinus readied himself, but there was no need. The rebel stopped in his tracks with a stunned look on his face, then fell forward at the centurion's feet with a dagger in his back. Marcus ran up from twenty steps away to pull it out.

"I'm getting better," he said. "That's the last of them, I think. Most already fled. We have a few arrests and a few dead. A pathetic attempt to usurp us. We'll have to get your eye checked out." He winced at the sight of it. Marcus was apprehensive to tell Longinus the next part. He swallowed hard and said, "There's something I need to show you."

"It can wait."

"I'm afraid it can't."

Marcus led Longinus to Kezia's body. When Longinus realized what Marcus was showing him, he forgot all about his injured eye. His heart filled up with an ache he had never known. The centurion collapsed to his knees and embraced the love of his life. Kezia's blue diamond eyes were still open, staring at nothing in particular. He kissed her and caressed her face. He looked at her bleeding wound.

"I told her to go back to the room," he said with a shaky voice. "Where's my son?"

But there was no answer. He looked around. Marcus was gone.

Pontius Pilate finally stepped onto his terrace to see what the commotion was about. He sipped his wine while examining the scene.

"Anything to be concerned about?" his wife asked from the bed.

"No, dear. Everything's under control. Only more evidence I'm in the wrong profession."

Pilate walked away from the terrace, placed his wine on a table, and then returned to bed with his wife. He began snoring almost instantly.

The Robbery

Ehud and Micah were still in the Upper City. They rode their stolen horses to the elite walled section where Caleb lived. The two fellow watchmen recognized them at once. Ehud and Micah were told they could come in so long as they had no plans to exit for a while. The watchmen were given strict orders to keep the gates locked till they received word the rebellion was over. Ehud and Micah agreed and smiled at their coworkers as they passed.

When the thieves turned the corner, they rode straight to the large olive tree that leaned against Caleb's wall. They dismounted their horses and climbed the tree. Ever so quietly, Micah readied his bow. Elijah, the older guard, was on duty. Micah conjured up all the memories of Elijah's cruelty while training under him many years prior. The taunting in front of others, the face-slapping when failing to perform a certain task. The memories still burned like fresh fire.

They saw Elijah standing on a basket and looking over the wall, presumably to check the status of the palace rebellion. Micah stared at his old mentor and pulled the bow back. He aimed at Elijah's head and released the arrow. It missed and went into the bushes. The sound startled Elijah. He immediately drew his sword. He turned toward the bushes, his back facing the olive tree.

"You idiot!" Ehud whisper-shouted at Micah. "Why do you always go for the smallest target? Why the head? Why the neck? Every single time. You always miss! Go for the bigger target. The chest perhaps. Have you thought about the chest? You know, the part where the heart is?"

"Relax. I've got him," Micah said calmly. He removed another arrow from his quiver and nocked it. He pulled the bow back and aimed at Elijah's neck. Elijah inspected the bushes, ready to attack something. Anything. He noticed an arrow sticking out of the ground. Alarmed, he turned around and opened his mouth to shout, wanting to alert the household. It was too late. Micah released the arrow. It pierced right through Elijah's throat. The guard made a low gurgling sound but nothing loud enough to alert anyone. In vain, he grabbed his neck as blood sprayed through his fingers. He collapsed to his knees as the life drained from him. The last thing he saw before closing his eyes forever was Micah climbing over the wall.

"You trained me well, didn't you?" said Micah to his old mentor. Ehud followed right behind. Both of them unsheathed their daggers. The two stood at each side of the door and waited for Ethan to start his shift.

Simon couldn't sleep. He left his wife in bed, came out to the reception room, and sat at a table. The light of the moon poured in through the open courtyard and garden. It was still dark enough for Simon to light an oil lamp. He heard the revolt taking place but wasn't all that concerned. These things happen and tend to be quickly dealt with. It was also beyond Caleb's walls, beyond the elite section of the Upper City. There was no reason to worry.

He stared at the mosaic floor. All the colored stones, marble, and glass pieces were arranged in such a way as to tell the Passover story of Moses leading the Israelites out of Egypt. The burning bush, Pharaoh, the devastating plagues, the Israelites passing through the Red Sea. Such intricate and detailed imagery.

Simon thought of his similar floor back home. He remembered when he and Caleb commissioned the work. How easy it was for them to pay the small fortune covering the artisan's travel expenses, labor, and materials. A thought occurred to Simon. Perhaps money was *his* Pharaoh and comfort *his* Egypt. Was Jesus of Nazareth right? Was he indeed a slave to his own wealth? Why were these thoughts still spinning around in his head? Why couldn't he simply count his blessings and move on?

"Abba," Joanna said in a voice far too awake for that hour. It made Simon jump in his chair.

"Joanna, don't startle your father like that. Why are you up? It's late."

"I can hear them fighting."

"Oh, you don't have to worry about that," said Simon. "We are behind walls behind walls. You should go back to bed."

Joanna climbed on Simon's lap instead.

"Is Ethan the strongest man in the world?" she asked.

"Why would you ask that?"

"That's what *he* told me."

"He did, did he? That Ethan says a lot of things. Little girls should not be spending time with such violent men."

"But I want to be as strong as him," she protested. "And he's my friend."

"And it's true," said a deep voice in the shadows. It was of course Ethan getting ready to start his shift. "I am the strongest man in the world."

"Giving your uncle a break?" Simon asked the young doorkeeper.

"It's about that time," Ethan said. "And your father's right, Joanna. No good can come from spending time with someone like me. You'll only become a mighty warrior able to defeat any enemy who dares harm you."

"Why Ethan?" Simon asked. "Why must you say these things? You'll only make her yearn for more of this boyish behavior."

Ethan laughed and said, "My apologies, sir. Your father is once again correct, Joanna. You should go back to sleep." He gave her a wink and a smile and walked away toward the barred door where Elijah was stationed just outside. Joanna jumped off her father's lap to follow him.

"Joanna, come back here this instant!" said Simon.

Ethan opened the door and saw Elijah on the dirt, his head resting in a pool of blood.

"Dod!" Ethan shouted and ran to the body.

But before Ethan could mourn his uncle properly, Ehud snuck up from behind him and opened his throat with the dagger. Joanna screamed and startled the two thieves who hadn't noticed the little girl run out behind the doorkeeper. Immediately, Micah grabbed a clump of her hair and pressed the dagger to her throat, careful not to cut her.

"Shut up, little girl or we'll do the same to you," he whispered in her ear. "You're going to help us get some money and then this will all be over."

He led her into the house and Ehud followed close behind, his dagger dripping Ethan's blood with each step.

Simon stood to his feet right away. He thought his heart may have stopped and struggled to speak for a moment.

"Let her go," he managed to finally blurt out. "She's my only daughter. She's just a little girl. What do you want? I'll give you anything. Please let her go."

The others in the home began to wake and pour into the reception room.

"What's going on?" Dinah said when she came out. She screamed at the sight of Micah with a dagger to her daughter's throat. The twins came out, and finally Caleb and his wife.

"Elijah! Ethan!" Caleb shouted. "Hurry! Get in here! There's trouble!"

"They're dead, Caleb," said Simon.

A wave of panic fell over Caleb, followed by fury.

"What is the meaning of this?" he asked the thieves. "Wait a minute... I know you two. You're both watchmen. You guard the walls."

"We've recently retired," Ehud said. "Give us what we want and no one gets hurt."

"Make one wrong move, any one of you," Micah added, "and the little girl dies. Are we clear?"

Joanna didn't say a word. She remembered Ethan telling her that people should never be feared. They can harm the body but never the soul. Bravely, she fought back tears.

"Money?" Caleb asked. "Is that what you want? Well, then you came to the wrong place. We don't keep any of it here. That would be foolish. We can't help you, unfortunately. Let my niece go and run along. I won't report you. You have my word."

"Oh, well if we have your word," Ehud said, "then we must be going now. After all, that's what we came for...your word."

"It's the truth!"

"Stop it, Caleb." Simon raised his hand to silence his brother. "The gold is under the floor."

"Simon!" Caleb said. "They'll keep coming back now. You idiot!"

"Nothing is worth Joanna's life," said Simon. "Or anyone else's life for that matter. You—" Simon pointed to Ehud. "Do you see where the Red Sea parts on the floor over there?" Ehud looked at the mosaic imagery on the floor and nodded when he found it. "Well, just as the Red Sea parts, so does the floor." Ehud stared at him, wondering if he could trust Simon's words.

"It's alright," Micah said. "I have his daughter. Check it out."

Ehud got down on his knees and discovered the tiles and mosaic pieces that showed the Isrealites walking on dry ground were removable, revealing a large open vault beneath it full of pouches and sacks of silver and gold. The eyes of the thieves widened in delight.

"It's far too much," Micah said. "One of you will open your gate for my partner to bring in our horses."

Simon looked at his brother.

"Fine," Caleb said reluctantly and did as instructed.

Ehud followed him to the property gate and brought in the horses, keeping a suspicious eye on Caleb the entire time.

"Load what you can," Micah told Ehud when he returned to the reception room. "It'll be enough to start a new life."

"What do you know about life?" said Caleb. "You're both cowards, not to mention traitors of your own people."

"Let them be," said Simon. "It's only money."

Caleb glared at his brother but didn't say a word.

When the horses were packed, Ehud came back into the home and said, "It's done."

"Very good," Micah said. "I'll let your daughter go as soon as I reach my horse. If any of you come after me, it'll be the last thing you do in this world. I'll force you to watch me kill every member of your family starting with her." Micah pulled on Joanna's hair a little tighter, making her wince. Then I'll finish you off as slowly as I can manage. Do we all understand?"

"You have our word," said Simon.

"They're giving us their word again," said Ehud with a laugh. "All these promises are quite touching."

"All I want is my daughter back. I have no interest in bringing you two to justice."

"Speak for yourself," Caleb muttered.

Ehud and Micah backed out of the home slowly. The dagger stayed close to Joanna's throat. She felt the sharpness of the blade. The two thieves walked around the unfortunate doorkeepers. Joanna shut her eyes when they met Ethan's feet. Ehud got on his horse and rode out of the property. Micah threw Joanna to the ground and did the same. Simon and Dinah then rushed out of the home to grab their daughter. They held each other close and wept, thankful to be alive.

The sound of more horses rushed past them. Simon opened his eyes.

"Wait! Where are you boys off to?" he shouted when he noticed his twins ride out of the property. He got up and ran outside the gate but they were too far. "Come back!" he shouted. "It's too dangerous!" He turned to his wife and said, "I need to get the boys! They'll get themselves killed."

Simon rushed Dinah and Joanna back inside the home, where Caleb was on his knees, looking down at the vault and counting how much was stolen.

"They must've taken half!" he said.

"Oh, who cares?" said Simon. "I have to get the twins." He ran to the stables and mounted a horse.

The Burial

Longinus stood to his feet. The blood in his throbbing left eye was beginning to clot. His thoughts were foggy with grief and shock. He knew he needed to find his son before anything else. He gently placed Kezia on the ground and went back to his private room in the barracks. He knocked in his rhythmic pattern, hoping the boy paid attention earlier. There was no response.

"Son, are you in there?" said Longinus. "Everything's alright. It's me."

The bar was finally lifted and the door opened. The boy hugged his father immediately and squeezed tight.

"Everything is not alright," the boy said.

"I'm so sorry, son. This wasn't supposed to happen."

"Father, your eye. You're hurt."

"Indeed. I'll look into it later. First things first."

Longinus brought his son outside to say goodbye to his mother. However, Kezia was not where he left her. He looked around and finally saw what was happening. Two soldiers were about to throw Kezia on top of a pile of bodies to be burned.

"Stop!" Longinus shouted. "Put her down right now!"

The frightened soldiers did as they were told and apologized for their error, though they knew not what it was.

Longinus was indeed brought up in the tradition of burning his dead. But he knew the Jews buried theirs. He also couldn't bear the thought of destroying Kezia's body.

The boy looked away when he saw his mother on the ground.

"Don't turn your face, boy," he said. "It's time to say goodbye."

The young Longinus knelt and kissed his mother on her forehead. He pulled the red windflower from her hair.

"What will we do with her?" he asked.

Longinus and his son brought Kezia to the one place he knew she felt accepted without question.

Nathan opened the door and fell to his knees when he saw the lifeless Kezia dangling from the centurion's arms.

"No," he said. "No, no, no. Why did she leave? Why did you take her from me? She was safe here, Longinus."

"I can't think of anyone better to bury her," Longinus said. He gently lay Kezia's body in front of Nathan, then kissed her forehead before rising to his feet. Nathan nodded, wiped away tears, and said, "I'll take care of it. But what of the boy? I can raise him. I really can. I'll do a good job."

The boy looked up at his father, wondering what he'd do. Longinus knew Nathan was more of a father to his son than *he* ever was.

"It's alright, Longinus," said Nathan, still crying. "You're a centurion. You're busy with your duties. Kezia never wanted *your* life for the boy. You know that."

Longinus said nothing for a moment. He stared at his son, then at Nathan and his battered face. Finally, he said, 'Nor do I want *your* life for my son. He's coming with me."

The boy looked at the red windflower, still in his hand, and placed it back in Kezia's hair.

"Dod, please bury her with this," he told Nathan. "Mother's favorite."

Longinus and the boy began their way back to the palace, as Nathan wept for losing the only two people he called family.

Escape

Ehud and Micah killed the two watchmen who refused to let them exit the Upper City's elite area. Pilate's and Herod's men were everywhere. All the gates of the city were now closed and heavily guarded. Ehud and Micah had no intention of escaping through any of them. They went to the only place they felt safe.

"What are you boys up to?" said Hannah, Micah's mother, when the two thieves entered her dilapidated home in the Lower City. They were shaking and nearly out of breath. Micah plopped down two of the stolen sacks on the earthen floor.

"Getting into trouble again?" she asked. "I hope you didn't have anything to do with all the fighting I heard."

"Mother," said Micah. "I need you to listen to me. I want you to have these."

"What is this?" she asked. When her son opened one of the sacks and she saw the glimmer of gold and silver coins, she pushed his hands away.

"Absolutely not!" she said. "Where did you get this? I'll have nothing to do with your thievery. May the Lord have mercy on you! Where did I go wrong with you? And Ehud, you should know better! Both of you should be ashamed of yourselves."

Micah was indeed ashamed of himself, but there was little time for self-reflection and rumination.

"Mother, take it," he said. "Live a better life. Ehud and I have to get out of here. You have no one. You need this."

Hannah noticed blood on his cloak.

"You're hurt," she said.

Micah looked away.

"The blood is not mine," he said.

She saw the blood on Ehud's hands as well and began to tremble. Through gritted teeth, she asked, "What have you done, boys?"

"Will you just take it?"

"The money is cursed! If you leave it, I'll give it all to the poor. Every last coin. I promise you that."

"Mother, you *are* the poor. I'm leaving the money right here. I trust you'll take care of yourself. We'll leave first thing in the morning. We need to rest for the night."

"Absolutely not!" said Hannah. "You'll leave right now. Get out!" She then slapped her son as hard as she could. Ehud backed away from her, afraid he was next.

"But Mother."

"Get out!"

"Come on, Micah," said Ehud. "They're following us, anyway. And Barabbas might come looking too."

"Barabbas?" said Hannah, repulsed by the very name. "How and why did you get mixed up with the likes of him? He's a scoundrel and a bandit pretending to fight for us. Who asked him to?"

"Who's following us?" asked Micah.

"Who do you think?" Ehud asked. "The people we just robbed, perhaps? I saw two of them on horses behind us. We lost them a couple of minutes ago. But they're out there. And Barabbas will be looking as well if he's not already dead."

"Get out! Get out! Get out!" shouted Hannah. She started to physically shove them out of her home. Ehud quickly grabbed an animal skin on the floor and rolled it up before Hannah grabbed him by his ear. "Stealing my rug too!" She took it from his hands, rolled it up, and started beating both of them with it.

"What's going on?" a neighbor came out to ask. She was another widow without a cent to her name. When she saw Ehud and Micah being thrown out, she said, "Oh, I see. Up to no good again. Do you need help, Hannah? I can beat them with *my* rug too."

"No, Ruth. I've got this, thank you."

Ehud managed to yank the rug from Hannah's hand and quickly shove it with the rest of his belongings. He and Micah got on their horses and rode off, leaving Hannah's shouts behind them.

It would be several hours later when the Lower City was sleepy enough for Hannah to quietly place the two sacks of gold and silver coins in front of Ruth's door. It was the only way she knew how to turn a curse into a blessing.

Barabbas had depended on Silvanus to let him out of Jerusalem, as they knew the riot would force the Romans to lock down the entire city. Now that his means of escape was dead, Barabbas was on his own. All he could think about was getting back to his wife and three children. They lived just beyond the city's walls. So close and yet impossible to reach. He rode past the gates to the elite residences, surprised to find two dead watchmen on the ground, each with their throats slit. He froze when he saw a few Roman soldiers patrolling and inspecting the situation. They froze as well when they saw Barabbas. He almost forgot he was dressed like a centurion. Barabbas pulled himself together to act like one and continued on.

The closest exit out of Jerusalem at this point was the Essene Gate. There was a crowd of soldiers gathered there, some belonging to Pilate, others to Herod. Lots of travelers were demanding the gates to be opened as they were frightened about the rebellion taking place. Barabbas needed a reason for the Romans to let him out. He swallowed hard, then galloped straight toward them, yelling, "Open the gates! Traitors have escaped! Orders from Pilate! I repeat. Open the gates! Traitors have escaped! Orders from Pilate!"

But the soldiers did nothing. They looked at one another. Barabbas realized his error immediately. He had blurted out the command in Greek, for he knew not a single word in Latin. He only knew Greek, Hebrew, and Aramaic. He reiterated the initial command. Again, the gates were not opened.

"Sir," one of the soldiers began in Greek to match his superior. "For whose sake are you speaking to us in Greek? "

Barabbas knew he couldn't get his way by reason. It was time to act. He'd seen Roman cruelty countless times. It was precisely why he became a Zealot in the first place. He got down from his horse and punched the questioning soldier in his stomach. Then he punched another nearby soldier in the face for absolutely no reason at all but to demonstrate force.

"I've been in this army for decades now," Barabbas said and

then escalated his voice, "and you dare question your superior about his speech? If I want to speak to you in Greek, I will speak to you in Greek or any other language for that matter. Is that understood? Now open the gate! A traitor dressed like one of you has escaped. Or perhaps it *is* one of you! Are you a traitor?" Barabbas grabbed one of Pilate's men by the neck while screaming this. He let the man go, mounted his horse, and said calmly in Greek, "Now open the gates. Traitors have escaped. Orders from Pilate."

The confused, terrified soldiers obliged, careful to beat back the people trying to run out behind Barabbas.

Ehud brought Micah to a secluded area between the Essene Gate and the Pool of Siloam. There was a drainage tunnel under the wall facing Hinnom Valley where the city's wastewater flowed out. They dismounted their horses.

"Now what?" said Micah. "And why did you steal my mother's rug? I should kill you for that."

"You left her with two sacks of gold and silver. She can buy whatever rug she wants now. We need it more than her." Ehud motioned for Micah to look at the drainage tunnel. "Well, here it is," he said. "It goes straight through to the other side of the wall... to freedom, my friend."

"No," Micah said. "I'm not crawling through that."

"Look," Ehud said. "No one is even guarding it. It's the only way."

"Why would they? It's disgusting! I'm not sure we can even fit through there. Why couldn't Barabbas get us clothing fit for a Roman soldier or centurion like him?"

"Maybe because he didn't trust us?" Ehud offered. "Can you blame him? Now let's go."

"You first," said Micah. "And how will we get all this money through? We can't carry it all and crawl through a river of—I can't even say it. This is an awful idea."

"You are a tender little baby," Ehud said. "You know that? That's exactly what you are. A baby. I should've killed you with the other watchmen. I'd be on my way to a life of luxury by now."

"I'd like to see you try," Micah rebutted. "Now go. It's your plan. Make it work. I'll follow behind."

Ehud unrolled the animal skin he took from Micah's mother and placed it on the fly-infested stream of urine and feces. He then started loading the sacks of silver and gold on the skin.

"I'll drag this through. You can take off your tunic and do the same."

"Then what?" Micah said. "We won't have horses on the other side. People will take one look at us...or perhaps one whiff of us and run the other way."

"We have daggers, don't we? We'll get new horses and a change of clothes one way or the other and we'll bathe in the river. Now stop being a baby already."

Reluctantly, Micah followed his partner's instructions. Ehud took a deep breath and entered the tunnel, crawling backward to drag the gold and silver. The weight of the sacks and pouches sunk the skin to the shallow bottom. Ehud couldn't tell if any of it fell off the skin. He'd inspect everything on the other side. It took far longer than he imagined.

Micah loaded his tunic and followed Ehud, wondering how in the world his life led him to this point, where he was willing to go through anything to not have to worry about money for once.

They reached the other side of the tunnel. It was a secluded area, hidden by trees and brush. A dirt road was only a few feet away. Both of them were dripping with filth, but neither cared. They were on the other side of the city's wall. Free. They piled the few sacks and pouches against the stone wall.

"Maybe we should count our blessings and leave the rest," Ehud suggested.

"I didn't murder tonight and crawl through Jerusalem's waste for nothing," Micah said. "We need to get all of it. No one is there. You said yourself, the tunnel isn't guarded. Who's the baby now?"

"Fine, we'll go." Ehud rolled up the animal skin. Micah led the way back this time.

Micah came out of the tunnel. He waved away the flies buzzing around him. He went to his horse and got two large pouches of gold.

"That's one of them," said the voice of a boy.

Startled, Micah turned and saw the twins accompanied by four Roman soldiers they had alerted about the robbery. The Romans always investigated crimes committed against the rich, hoping for a reward if they captured the criminal.

Ehud heard the commotion from inside the tunnel and slowly

made his way back to the other side.

Simon finally caught up to the twins.

"My boys!" he said, nearly out of breath.

"Father, we found them," his son said.

"One of them, at least," the other added.

"Did this man steal your money?" a soldier asked Simon.

"And killed our guards!" the boys shouted excitedly. "He even put a dagger to our young sister's throat."

"He was a lot cleaner a few minutes ago," said Simon. "But I believe that's him. I do hope you catch the other one."

"Probably on the other side of the wall," the soldier said. "Or perhaps still under it. Either way, we'll get him."

Micah had no protest. It was over. He looked at the two pouches of gold in his hand, then dropped them. He collapsed to his knees.

"Get up. I'm not touching you." The soldier threw a rope over Micah, then pulled tight to bind his arms. The other three soldiers surrounded him. They took turns kicking him forward.

"What will happen to him now?" Simon asked.

"We'll bring him to the pit. Pilate will have him executed soon enough, I imagine. Don't you worry, sir." Then looking at Micah, he shouted, "Were you part of the rebellion as well?" He gave Micah a hard and swift kick to the chest. He fell to the ground, gasping for air.

Simon stared at the feces-covered pouches of gold and then at his two sons, wondering if God was teaching him a lesson about value that night.

One of the soldiers saw Simon staring and said, "We'll clean this money right up for you and deliver it in the morning, along with the rest of it. Straight to your door, sir. No problem at all."

Simon didn't trust that would happen, but he also didn't care. His family was safe.

Ehud made it back to the other side of the tunnel. He didn't have all the money he wanted, but he no longer had a partner to split everything two ways. It was enough to start a new life. That's all that mattered.

"Goodbye old friend," he whispered. "We had a good run."

Now free, Barabbas could breathe and relax, but he didn't want to get too comfortable. He made a left, intending to ride halfway around the wall to get his family and find somewhere to hide for a little while. He had a cousin in nearby Bethany. It was close, but far enough for the time being.

But then Barabbas saw something peculiar: a man covered in the city's waste emerging from the drainage tunnel. He squinted. Then his heart burned with fury when he realized who it was. Barabbas brought his horse to a halt. He jumped off and drew his sword.

Ehud shuttered at the sight of a centurion.

"I hope you got enough money to pay God for your sins, traitor," said Barabbas, as he threw his crested helmet to the ground. "I counted on you two."

"Oh, Barabbas, it's you," said Ehud. "Get your head out of the clouds. You can't beat the Roman army. Ever. You're wasting your time. *I* know that. Micah knows that. Everyone knows that. Everyone but you, that is."

"Speaking of which," Barabbas said. "Where is your partner in crime? Has Micah abandoned you already?"

Ehud said nothing.

"Dead?" Barabbas ventured another guess. "Or did he already get caught?"

Ehud stared at Barabbas and said, "Enough…you have your sword out. I have my dagger. Let's settle this. What do you want to do? Let us not waste any more precious time."

"I should have the money you stole from god-knows-where. It's only right for your betrayal. Hand it over and I'll leave you alone. Forever."

"You're mistaking me for someone who's frightened. You want this money? Fight for it."

Through gritted teeth, Barabbas said, "Gladly." He charged Ehud with his sword. Ehud dodged in such a way as to make Barabbas lose his footing and fall headfirst into the wastewater. Ehud laughed and unsheathed his dagger. He jumped on top of Barabbas. The two former friends rolled around in filth and anger. They were almost of equal strength. Neither heard when the Roman soldiers came up and surrounded them. They finally stopped fighting and looked around.

"Well a lot of good this did us," Ehud said.

Marcus got off his horse and stood over Barabbas.

"I know someone who would very much like to meet you," he said. "Barking orders in Greek? You almost pulled it off too. You really did. Not bad, I have to admit. Not bad at all. My men told me you put on a great show."

"Well," Ehud interrupted, "I have to thank you fine gentlemen for saving me from this bandit. If you'll excuse me now, I'll be on my way."

"Don't you move!" Marcus said. "My men already caught your friend on the other side. You'll both be joining him in the pit." Then looking at one of the soldiers, he commanded, "Bind them. Let's go. Don't forget the money bags in the bushes."

PART TWO

The Doctor

Back in the room, the boy was quiet. His entire life had changed in an instant. He suddenly realized he knew very little about his father. Meanwhile, the physician was not happy with what he saw.

"I'm afraid you'll never see again in this eye," he told Longinus.

"You won't tell Pilate?"

"Your secret is safe with me. However, you do realize he'll probably notice it himself. You can't hide this."

"Let me worry about that," said Longinus.

"Shall I begin then? First, I'll remove the eye with—"

"Remove my eye?"

"But of course," the physician said. "No use in keeping an eye that doesn't work."

"I don't want you removing my eye. Isn't there anything else?"

"All I can do is prevent infection. I can't promise I won't be coming back in a few days to take your eye out. We can see how it goes. Why not get it over with now?"

Longinus glared at the doctor with his one good eye.

"As you wish." The physician put the hook and forceps back in his medical supply satchel and took out a long needle to pierce and drain the wound.

Longinus advised the doctor to strap his arms and hands to the chair before he began. This ensured Longinus would not strike him out of pure instinct. Killing anyone who caused him or his loved ones pain was so deeply ingrained in him, that he didn't trust himself.

The physician was used to such protocols and did as the centurion suggested. Longinus was already stabbed in the eye once that night, but the second time by the doctor felt somehow worse. The boy winced as his father screamed and contorted, strapped in the chair. Afterward, the doctor applied a vinegar mixture to cleanse the wound.

Longinus sat there panting. Helpless. Beads of sweat dripped from the top of his head. He barely had time to recover before the next procedure began.

"Abba," the boy said with great concern when the doctor heated the end of a hawthorn stick in the flame of an oil lamp.

"This will stop the bleeding and seal the wound," the doctor said, hoping to put the boy at ease. It did not. "You don't want your father getting infected, do you?"

"It's alright son," said Longinus. "I've faced tougher enemies than pain."

The end of the stick glowed red. The boy watched the dark smoke form a trail in the air, as the doctor walked to his father. The boy turned his head at that point. He couldn't bear any more of it. Longinus roared from the pain and wept. The boy covered his ears. Then all went silent. Longinus passed out.

He awoke shortly after the doctor applied a poultice of crushed herbs soaked in vinegar to the ruined eye. He wrapped strips of linen on the centurion's head to hold it in place.

"Don't worry, boy," the doctor said. "Your father will be fine. Just keep to his right side, so he can see you."

There was a familiar knock on the door. The doctor left the centurion and his son to tend to other soldiers injured during the revolt. He was greeted by Marcus on his way out. Longinus took deep and steady breaths to get through the pain.

Marcus said hello to the boy and asked how he was doing. The boy didn't answer.

"And what about you?" he asked his father.

"I've been better, Marcus." Now unstrapped from his chair, Longinus started gulping down entire cups of wine.

"Well…I have a gift for you. It won't give you your sight back, unfortunately."

"Will it bring Kezia back to life?" Longinus asked.

"No. It won't do that either," Marcus replied.

"Then I can't say I'm very much interested in your gift at the moment. I need to rest. We'll talk in the morning."

"Silvanus was number ninety-nine, correct?"

Longinus grunted.

"Well, I've found number one hundred for you."

"I've fought enough tonight, Marcus."

"It's the man who killed Kezia."

Longinus finally turned to face his trainee.

"I saw when it happened," Marcus continued. "It was a rebel disguised as a centurion. I caught him outside the wall fighting with another man who was arrested for stealing and murder."

Longinus stood to his feet.

"Take me to him."

"We can wait till morning," Marcus said. "He's not going anywhere. I had my men put him in the pit. I only wanted to inform you. You need your rest tonight."

"Take me to him now."

Marcus saw how determined Longinus was and said, "Very well."

The young Longinus wanted to follow his father and Marcus but was told to stay in the room.

"Bar the door. You know the knock," his father said.

"Don't leave me alone," the boy said.

"Do as you're told. I'll be back. There's nothing to worry about. You're safe."

"That's what you said before he killed her."

This pierced right through his father's soul. Longinus was not sure which hurt worse, his eye or his heart. He said nothing and left with Marcus. The boy barred the door as instructed.

Gratitude

Simon and his sons returned to Caleb's palace and put the horses in the stables. When they went inside the home, Dinah and Joanna ran up to them.

"Oh, thank God!" Dinah said. The family of five crashed into each other's arms.

"What happened?" Leah asked.

The boys broke away from their family's embrace and were so excited to recount their adventure of chasing after the thieves. They were talking over one another and finishing each other's sentences. They spoke of finding Roman soldiers and convincing them to follow them to the Lower City where the thieves rode off to, and how they couldn't find them for a few minutes. Then they noticed two horses not moving anywhere near the Pool of Siloam. That's when they found one of the men.

Caleb was still on the ground counting the money that wasn't stolen, trying to figure out exactly what was missing. The last part of the story got his attention.

"They were caught?" he asked with excitement in his voice. "This is great news! Did you get all of the money back? Tell me you got the money back."

"The Romans will clean and return it by morning," said Simon.

"Clean it? What on earth are you talking about?"

Simon was exasperated at his brother's fixation on the money and found it grossly inappropriate given their lives were spared and peace had been restored to their family. Moreover, little Joanna was just fine, trauma aside.

"The thieves were trying to escape through a drainage tunnel," Simon explained. "The money was dragged through the city's filth. So the soldiers offered to clean the money and return it by morning."

Caleb threw his hands in the air and said, "And you believed them? Brother, they are greedy, good-for-nothing Romans. Their word means nothing. They're worse thieves than the men who robbed us. We may never see that money again. Certainly not all of it!"

"My little girl is alive. That's all that matters."

"Simon, you know I love Joanna like my own daughter. I would be ruined if anything happened to her. But thank God she's alive! She's fine. Look at her."

Simon looked at Joanna, still in her mother's arms. He smiled.

"Meanwhile," Caleb continued, "some of our wealth has been stolen. We don't know if we'll ever get it back and you're acting like you don't care."

"I don't."

This response shocked and silenced Caleb. He stared at his brother in disbelief. He knew something was broken and would never be the same.

Simon sent his boys to sleep and brought his wife and Joanna back to their room. Dinah never wanted to let her go again. They said a goodnight prayer together thanking God for his mercy and grace.

Leah kissed Caleb's forehead and went to bed as well. Caleb stayed up a little longer to finish counting.

The Pit

The pit was underneath the governor's palace. It was a fitting nickname for such a dank, dark, and desperate dungeon. There were a few prisons throughout the city, but most traitors, insurrectionists, and men who committed crimes generally worthy of execution were brought to the pit to await trial. It smelled of vomit, feces, and mildew. The air was cold and the floor was wet. The rats always outnumbered the inmates.

Micah sat on the ground, chained against the stone wall with the rest of the insurrectionists who were caught, along with some prisoners who were already there. Many of them were terminally wounded from the fight, praying to die before their imminent executions. A few hopeful prisoners were working on their explanations for Pilate. *No, you don't understand Governor. I was simply passing through and one of your soldiers confused me for a rebel. I actually think you're a just ruler. Why would I want to free myself from your goodness? This has been one huge misunderstanding.*

Micah had not even been in the pit for more than forty-five minutes when Barabbas and Ehud were brought in.

"Ah, my other friend-turned-traitor," Barabbas said when he saw him. "You're lucky I'm in chains."

"If any of us were lucky," Ehud said, "we wouldn't be in a dungeon, now would we?"

"Shut up you two!" yelled the guard bringing them in. They chained Ehud and Barabbas to the wall, not far from Micah. Ehud waited for the Romans to leave and lock the gate behind them before whispering.

"Let's put our differences behind us," he said. "I'm sure some Romans on our side can get us out for the right price."

"Why would any Roman risk his life for us at this point?" asked Barabbas. "What can we offer them now? We've already paid who we can pay."

"We may have dropped some silver and gold in the tunnel. If we can just get out of here, we'll have enough to pay whoever we need to."

"Gold in a tunnel," Barabbas scoffed. "Here I am thinking we're all in this together. Not for temporary gain, but to change the future of our nation, our people. Give a better life to our children. But all you want is money. You'll betray anyone, kill anyone, and crawl through anything to get it. I hope it was worth it. Look where it got you. I'll never trust you two again. I thought we were friends. After all this time. All this planning. And yet you expect me to work with you to escape this hell hole."

"You two are wasting your time," Micah said. "It's over. Accept your fate. Prepare to meet God. There is no escaping this."

"The mute finally speaks," Ehud said. "And loud enough for even the guards to hear. Tell me, Micah, what on earth do we have to lose? Don't you think we should at least try to get out of here?"

"No," he answered, more quietly this time. "I don't."

Neither Barabbas nor Ehud said anything to this. The reality of the situation was too hard to bear.

"My wife and children probably think I'm dead," said Barabbas.

"I'm not sure if my mother cares what happened to me," Micah added.

"Two big babies, the both of you," said Ehud.

"Barabbas, our fearless leader!" shouted another prisoner. "I heard you managed to kill a whore. Congratulations, Jerusalem is finally free!"

The prisoners who weren't crying or moaning in pain chuckled at this.

"Long live the whore killer!"

Barabbas said nothing. The group of them were silenced when they heard the gates open up.

"They've caught some more of us, I suppose," Ehud muttered.

Much to their chagrin, they shuttered at the sight of a centurion and high-ranking official.

Barabbas recognized both of them and his heart sank.

Number One Hundred

"That's him," Marcus pointed. "I was told his name is Jesus Barabbas. Your one-hundredth kill. You can finally retire."

Longinus walked up to him and knelt to be at eye level. He stared at him with his one good eye without saying a word and did his best to contain his disgust from the stench, though it provided a brief distraction from his throbbing pain.

Barabbas stared at the linen wrapping on the centurion's head and noticed the brownish-red stain over the left eye. "What do you want with me?" he asked.

"Oh, lots of things," Longinus answered. "But to sum it up in a single word…justice. That's what I want from you and that's what you'll give me."

"Justice?" Barabbas asked. "I'm not the one who injured you. That was probably Silvanus."

"Oh, but you are," Longinus said. "You have injured me. Much worse than my eye."

Barabbas had no idea what he was talking about.

"The woman you killed," Longinus said.

"Yes?" Barabbas said, his voice trembling a bit now.

The prisoner who was taunting Barabbas earlier said, "What are the chances? That was *his* whore. You've done it now Barabbas."

Without uttering a word, Longinus walked up to that prisoner and smacked him unconscious. Then he walked back to Barabbas.

"That woman happened to be my son's mother," he said.

"But she was a Jew," Barabbas said. "It was an accident. I didn't mean it. I'm so sorry."

"Who did you *mean* to kill?" asked Longinus.

Barabbas had no answer.

"Relax, I'm not going to kill you," Longinus continued. "I'm not even going to torture you. So no, Marcus, I won't be retiring yet. The cross will be much worse than anything I can do to him. I'll nail you to the wood, myself. I'll watch you for as long as it takes. I want to see you struggle to breathe until it becomes impossible. If I get bored or grow impatient, I'll bring a vat of honey with me to cover you. A treat for the flies."

"I wonder if crows or vultures like honey," wondered Marcus. "Ooh, you should put it on his bits to find out. That will be a great laugh."

"I wouldn't dream of robbing you from such a just execution," continued Longinus. "But I'm certainly going to watch and enjoy every minute of it." The centurion stood to his feet. "Pilate should be formally sentencing all of you to death shortly. Have a good night, everyone. Pleasant dreams, Barabbas."

Longinus left without another word. He didn't even wait for Marcus who stayed behind to take a head count and note the injuries. He needed this information to report to Pilate.

Marcus could barely see anyone's face. The pit was dark and smelled horrid. He spent a lot of time covering his nose with his arm.

When he finished counting the men and noting their physical condition, he quickly turned around to leave.

"Marcus," a familiar voice called out to the decurion before he made it out of the cell. Marcus turned around to see where the voice was coming from. He scanned the prisoners till he noticed Felix chained in a corner.

"Felix?" Marcus said, utterly shocked. He ran up to him, "Oh, Felix, what have you done?"

"We had to try," Felix whispered.

"But why?" Marcus whispered back. "What was accomplished? Look at you."

"Freedom is not free, my friend."

"But you *were* free. Why take up the cause of the Jews? For money? Whatever they paid you, was it worth it?"

"We're not as free as you think, Marcus. Our every move is dictated. That is not freedom. Nobody paid me anything. I

The Last Converts of Christ

volunteered. And yes it was worth it. The chance to do my part in ushering in a new kingdom."

Marcus noticed Felix was wounded under his rib cage. He was still bleeding.

"I'll send a doctor," Marcus said.

Felix laughed through the pain, then groaned immediately after doing so.

"For what?" he said. "You already know what they do to traitors. Let me be. If I'm lucky, my injury will kill me before they strangle or crucify me, whatever fancies Pilate when my trial comes."

Marcus leaned in toward Felix's ear to speak low enough so none of the other prisoners could hear.

"I'm going to help you escape," he said.

"No, Marcus. Let me be," Felix whispered back. "My time has come and it's alright."

Marcus said nothing. He stood upright, resolved in what he needed to do, then left the prison.

Palm Sunday

Later the next day, Longinus and Marcus stood before Pilate in his private chambers among several other Roman officials. They were to give him a full report of the rebellion the night before.

"How many casualties?" Pilate asked.

"We burned twenty-three bodies before dawn," one official said. "Eight of them Romans, the rest were rebels—Zealots we presume, though we can't be certain. There may be civilians among the dead as well."

"Did any of the rebels escape?"

"Most of them, actually. They fled almost immediately, sir."

"Cowards. How many are in the pit right now?" Pilate sat in his chair aimlessly flipping a coin with Caesar's inscription on it.

"Fifty-four in the pit," Marcus answered. "Some of whom were already there awaiting trial. Seven rebels appear mortally wounded, sir. I don't think they'll make it to trial."

"Always a shame, isn't it? The weak offenders being denied proper justice. Life is not fair. Do we have information about these rebels? Any names?"

"There was one disguised as a centurion," Marcus said. "His name is Jesus Barabbas. I caught him and two of his personal associates, who had stolen from the house of Caleb the spice merchant."

"Insurrection *and* thievery," Pilate said. "All in one night. Interesting."

Another official spoke up and said, "And murder, sir. Upper City watchmen were killed as well as some of our soldiers. Two were lit on fire. I've also been told this Barabbas killed a whore. Isn't that right, Marcus?"

Marcus wanted to save Longinus from anger and disgrace as quickly as possible. "She was an innocent woman," he said, "as well as a mother. I witnessed the murder, myself."

Longinus hated people reducing the love of his life to a profession he had every intention of saving her from. He burned with anger. But in the presence of Pilate, he held his tongue.

"How many traitors?" Pilate asked.

Marcus froze.

The first official spoke up.

"Again, it's hard to tell, sir. Many rebels were disguised as *us*. Perhaps traitors were in disguise as well."

"Perhaps," Pilate agreed. "But we'll sniff them out. We always do."

"Silvanus seems to have been the main culprit," Longinus said. "He's been taken care of."

"Silvanus?" Pilate said incredulously. "Are you sure? I don't think I had a centurion in my entire army who's served longer. He was on the brink of retirement. You must be mistaken."

"I assure you," Longinus answered. "He helped two rebels light those soldiers on fire, which initiated the rebellion. I saw Silvanus kill one of our men with my own eyes."

The word *eyes* caught Pilate's attention. He stood from his chair and walked over to Longinus.

"Remove your helmet," he commanded.

Reluctantly, Longinus did as he was told.

"Lift the linen. I want to see what you're working with here."

Longinus obeyed. Pilate grimaced at the sight of melted flesh in place of a left eye. He leaned in closer to inspect.

"What is your name?" Pilate asked.

"Longinus, sir."

"I'll never remember that. Did Silvanus do this to you? How bad is it?"

"A mere scratch," Longinus told Pilate, forgetting to answer the first question. His entire head was throbbing with pain.

"That's one disgusting scratch," said Pilate. "Can you still perform your duties or shall I find your replacement at once? Who's ready to be a centurion here?"

"I'm fine," answered Longinus, not giving time for anyone to take Pilate's offer. "I can perform my duties as well as before my injury. Perhaps even better."

"We shall see," said Pilate. "I just hope *you* can see."

There were a few scattered chuckles in the room.

"Well, don't be shy," said Pilate. "It was a joke. Laugh!"

At once, all the Roman officials—save Longinus and Marcus—began roaring in laughter.

"Alright, that's enough!" said Pilate. "I'm not here to be your entertainment. Do me a favor—what was your name again?"

"Longinus."

"Longinus, yes. Please cover that back up and tend to your oozing wound tomorrow. No need to disgust your subordinates with that monstrosity of a face. You can resume your duties the following day."

Longinus bowed his head in gratitude.

Another official spoke up.

"Sir, peace has been restored in the city," he said. "It's as though nothing happened. The rebellion was an utter failure."

Pilate nodded in approval. Just then, one of his advisors entered.

"There's a bit of commotion happening by the Temple Mount," he reported.

"Commotion? What kind of commotion? Another attack?"

Pilate walked out onto his terrace, which overlooked most of Jerusalem.

"No, sir," said the advisor. "Someone has entered through the Golden Gate. A man named Jesus, a rabbi of sorts. The people are shouting praises and laying down cloaks and palm branches before him like he's a king. The entire city is talking about him."

"A rabbi, you say? There are hundreds of rabbis here. Why the uproar?"

"Some say he's a prophet, a miracle worker."

Pilate scoffed and said, "Nonsense. These people will believe anything, won't they?"

"I've heard reports of him causing the blind to see, the lame to walk, and even raising a dead man back to life."

At this, Pilate began to laugh uncontrollably. The officials in the room took their cue to do the same.

"Did they see him flying in the clouds as well?" Pilate joked. "Or perhaps walk on water, or juggle a couple of dragons? People are such idiots. They truly are. How much does he charge for his miracles? Can I afford to hire him for my own amusement?"

"Very humorous, sir."

"Tell me if he had anything to do with the insurrection last night. Does he want to *miraculously* take my place?"

"Not to my knowledge, sir."

"Then keep an eye on him. I wouldn't bother with him too much. I swear to you, these religious fanatics are going to be the death of me. Everyone is dismissed."

The Decision

Simon and his family rested the entire day after the robbery. It took quite the emotional toll on them. He and Caleb hadn't spoken to one another since the night before.

Family members of Elijah and Ethan had come in the afternoon to collect their bodies for burial. When they left, Caleb poured water on the blood-stained dirt and moved the mud around to rid himself of the carnage. He and Leah mourned deeply, as the uncle and his nephew were like family to them. Little Joanna watched from a distance when Ethan was loaded onto a cart and taken away from the property.

It was just after sunset when two Roman guards came to the exquisite home. Being that Caleb had not hired any new doorkeepers yet, he had to tend to the gated entrance himself. Simon was sitting in the garden at the time and rose to his feet at the sight of soldiers. He walked toward his brother to join him at the gate.

"As promised," the Roman said. "Here's your money. All cleaned from the filth. Have a good day." The soldier handed Caleb two pouches of silver coins, then turned to leave.

"Excuse me," Caleb said. The soldiers turned around. "Where's the rest of it?"

"The rest of what?" the soldier asked.

"The money. Where is the rest of my money? Much more than this was stolen. This is only silver. There were many pouches and sacks of gold, not to mention much more silver than this. I want it all back this instant."

"Sorry, this is all we retrieved. Have a good day."

"No, you are lying," Caleb said. "Nearly half my money was stolen and you are going to return it."

The Roman soldiers looked at one another.

"Like we said, this is all we recovered. Maybe the thieves hid the rest of it."

"Maybe *you* hid the rest of it!" Caleb said. Fury mounting within him by the second.

"Brother, let them be," said Simon. "It's only money."

This caused Caleb to turn on his brother. He got up in his face, grabbed his tunic near the neck, and said, "Only money? Is that all it is? How many hours did it take to accumulate it? How many travels? How many transactions? What's wrong with you?" He tackled Simon to the ground and began shaking him.

Meanwhile, the Roman soldiers left the brothers alone to quarrel and roll around in the dirt.

"Brother, they're gone," said Simon. "Get off of me already." Caleb looked up to discover Simon was right. The soldiers had left. He began to weep.

"We're never getting our money back now," Caleb said. He got up and walked back inside the palace. Simon stayed in the garden for a while, questioning his entire life. The wives saw the altercation but kept quiet. Finally, Simon finished feeling sorry for himself and got up from the ground where his brother left him.

They ignored one another the following morning. Late in the afternoon, Simon went to seek the Lord in the temple. He needed to hear from God directly.

When he arrived, he was completely dumbfounded by what was happening. People were shouting and cursing. There were overturned tables and benches and broken dove cages. Cattle and sheep were roaming about. Scattered coins were all over the ground and everyone was scurrying about to gather them up.

"What happened here?" he asked one of the temple merchants.

"Jesus of Nazareth did this! Then he had the nerve to start preaching to us about God's house being a house of prayer, not a den of thieves. He cost me a fortune today!"

"Jesus, you say? Where is he now? Where did he go?"

"No idea. But I hope he doesn't come back."

Simon pondered everything that happened. Suddenly it all

became clear. He understood what he needed to do.

He returned to Caleb's palace and proudly announced to the family, "I've decided to give away all of our wealth to the poor and follow God. I need to find Jesus tomorrow."

The children looked at one another, wondering what was wrong with their father.

"Maybe you should lie down for a bit," his wife suggested.

"Your brother has gone crazy," Leah whispered to Caleb.

"If that's how you feel," Caleb told Simon, "then when you get back home, send a ship with all your money to me. I'll take it off your hands since it's such a burden to you. As far as I'm concerned, you owe me anyway. It's your fault half of my money is gone now."

Simon started to laugh and said, "I love you, Caleb. I truly do. You will earn more money. I promise you. But the poor need it much more than you do, and that's who I will give it to."

Caleb shook his head at this and left the room.

Complaints

Later that evening, Pilate's advisor came into his private chambers and said, "Sir, some Sadducees are complaining about Jesus."

"Jesus?" Pilate asked. "The whore killer?"

"No, sir. The one I told you all the people have gone mad over."

"The magician?"

"Miracle worker, they say."

"Miracles are illusions. Are they not?"

"I suppose."

"That makes him a magician. A performer of tricks. Nothing more. What has he done?"

"Some of the religious leaders mentioned he caused quite a bit of fuss at the temple today, throwing over the tables of the money changers and merchants, even whipping items this way and that."

"Did you say whipping?"

"Yes, sir."

"I'd like to whip some of them, myself. Why would this concern me?"

"They want you to do something."

"Do something?" Pilate asked. "Fine. I'll do something. Tell them the next time this Jesus wants to whip them, I shall join him and the two of us will have a marvelous time whipping them together. Tell them *that's* what I have decided to do."

"Very well, sir." The advisor turned to leave.

"I'm kidding, you idiot. Come back here."

The advisor returned.

"Tell them they can deal with this Jesus on their own," Pilate said. "Unless he is claiming to be a king and intends to take us over, he isn't my problem. I don't care if he whips every last one of them out of town. He'd be saving me the trouble. Their problem, not mine. Leave me alone now."

A Wound and an Argument

Nearly two full days had passed since the failed revolt at the governor's palace. When Marcus finally located the same physician who treated Longinus, he brought him down to the pit to examine Felix in the middle of the night.

"Where were you all this time?" Marcus whispered in the doctor's ear, as they walked briskly.

"Treating soldiers, sir. Many were injured."

"Well, my friend might be dead by now. It'll be your fault if he is."

Marcus knew this wasn't true, but the doctor was an easy and powerless person to blame.

On the way, Marcus took note of the guards he'd have to inconspicuously get past to help Felix escape. It didn't look good. Aside from the prison commander, there were also two guards in charge of the inner cell. There would also be a lot of people throughout the halls of the Praetorium who may very well question why Marcus was walking around with a half-naked injured man. He'd need a pretense.

The doctor gagged when they entered the pit. The stench was unbearable. Aside from feces, vomit, and body odor, there was the aroma of imminent death that hung in the air almost thick enough to wade through. They kicked rats as they made their way to Felix in the dimly lit dungeon.

"My apologies, doctor," said Marcus, briefly uncovering his nose to speak. "I know you normally don't have to make visits down here."

"Never," the doctor said. "Let's make this quick, shall we? Where is he?"

They found Felix sweating profusely with a fever. He showed the doctor the stab wound.

"I...I..." stuttered Felix, "I thought I told you to leave me alone, Marcus. Why are you here? Who's *he*?"

"He's a physician," replied Marcus. "He's just going to take a look at you. Try to relax."

"I thought I told you there's no use. Let me die of my wounds. It will be far greater than what they'll do to me if I make it to trial."

"He's right, you know?" said the doctor.

"Be quiet," said Marcus. "Doctor, please remember to whisper down here and speak only in Latin. We don't need the attention of the other inmates. How does it look?"

The doctor sighed and said quietly, "It's infected. It's also still bleeding. It must be deep. Not good at all. I can clean and suture it. But there are no guarantees. Your friend is correct. If you care at all about him, why heal him only to let him die a much more torturous and agonizing death?"

Marcus had no intention of revealing his rescue plans. He was too scared to trust someone he barely knew with such treasonous notions.

"See what you can do," he answered.

The physician opened his medical supply satchel and did what he could. Felix moaned throughout the entire procedure.

Marcus dismissed the doctor and instructed one of the prison guards to lead him out of the pit. He waited till he heard the gates shut and lock before speaking to Felix.

"I'll let you rest," Marcus whispered. "You'll need your strength."

"You're making a big mistake," Felix said. "I've made my choice and will take whatever consequence it brings."

"And I've made my choice," said Marcus.

"Hey, why do you keep tending to that man and no one else?" shouted a prisoner in Aramaic from the other side of the cell. "Many of us need medical attention. Help us!"

Marcus understood the gist of what he said. But he ignored the man and simply left the pit without another word.

On his way out, Marcus heard that same prisoner shouting over and over behind him, "What's so special about him?"

When the decurion was gone, the shouting inmate said to Felix, "You two are up to something, aren't you?"

"Death is the only thing I'm up to," said Felix in a weak and exhausted voice. "I assure you that."

The man grumbled bitterly, then turned his attention toward Barabbas, who he couldn't see from his vantage point.

"This is all your fault, Barabbas! I know you're in here somewhere."

Barabbas stayed quiet. He had been trying to listen to Felix and Marcus's conversation but could not understand any of it. Nor were they talking loud enough if he could. Barabbas didn't know everyone involved. He knew there were several Roman traitors but had no idea who they were except Silvanus, who personally hired those he trusted to help carry out the revolt. Felix was one of those men, though he accepted no payment for the job.

"You and all your speeches," the prisoner went on. "You know, I believed you. I did. I was convinced nothing could stop us. *The Lord was on our side,* you said. *How could we fail?* Well, look at us now, Barabbas. The half-hearted who escaped are enjoying time with their families right now. Meanwhile, your most devoted are chained to walls, on the brink of torture and death. If this is what it's like to have the Lord on our side, I can't imagine the devil being much worse."

"Blasphemy!" Barabbas finally shouted. "Are we not to accept both good and bad from the Lord? Perhaps your attitude toward the things of God has contributed to this mess?"

"It could always be worse, my friend," added Micah, who had been listening to this exchange.

"You have no right to speak," said Barabbas. "You abandoned your post. Perhaps we would have succeeded if you hadn't been so selfish."

"Oh, shut up Barabbas!" said Ehud. "The plan was doomed from the start. That's the only reason we abandoned you. Not only that, but you seem to have forgotten that we indeed started the rebellion. We came through with Silvanus."

"Yes, and then you left," said Barabbas. "You left me to fight on my own."

"It's the Roman army! I don't even know how many came with Pilate. But did they not outnumber and overwhelm you in minutes? Did not Herod's men join them almost immediately, which is exactly what I expected? If you were too blind at the time, then forgive *me* for seeing the truth. But I didn't change anything. Either way, I still would've ended up dead or in here."

"I should've listened to my wife," the bitter prisoner added. "She warned me about you, Barabbas. About all you Zealots. But I didn't listen."

"You can say '*all you Zealots*' all you want," said Ehud. "Like it or not you're one of us now. You made your choice. Nobody forced you to do a thing."

"I hope my mother will use the gold to make a better life for herself," said Micah.

"You truly are a baby," Ehud scolded. "Even now. Unbelievable."

The Council of Thirteen

Long after most had gone to sleep, a secret meeting took place. The high priest, Joseph ben Caiaphas, held it at his palace in the Upper City. It was not the first of its kind. However, he was now determined to vote on a final resolution. He invited his usual twelve members of Jerusalem's wealthy and religious elite. These were prominent Pharisees and Sadducees, temple officers, and a few select representatives of the Sanhedrin. Normally, they did not all get along, and rarely did they unanimously agree on anything, but they were willing to put aside their differences to solve the problem of Jesus. Sitting next to Caiaphas was his father-in-law Annas, who was once High Priest himself and still honored as such. Caiaphas often consulted with Annas for sensitive decisions. Also seated at the table were Jonathan and Theophilus, both sons of Annas. Then there were Ithamar, Kish, Gamaliel the Elder and his son Simeon, David, Benjamin, and Solomon the scribe. Lastly, there were Nicodemus and Joseph of Arimathea, the wealthiest men in the council, both of whom happened to be secret followers of Jesus.

And so gathered together in the large room were some of the high priest's most trusted allies. People he could generally rely on to act in Jerusalem's best interest. This was particularly true about mitigating any problems with the potential to complicate the delicate relationship between the Jews and Romans. Collectively, he referred to this secret group as the *Council of Thirteen*. The odd number proved useful in avoiding split decisions.

"Thank you all for meeting with me once again," began

Caiaphas. "Hopefully, this evening will be fruitful. We are now in need of an immediate and permanent solution to our problem. Jesus gains in popularity with each passing day. The crowds grow larger and larger. And with all these visitors in the city, his reputation will only spread far and wide. The people cling to every word he speaks."

"Words that challenge our own, I may add," said Jonathan. "He questions our authority in the synagogue. He seems to question the very priestly order that has been established for generations. I've been told he even questions the law."

"As far as I can tell," said Caiaphas, "he is guilty of even the greater sin of blasphemy. There is only one way to handle a blasphemer."

"We are not legally able to do that," said Gamaliel the Elder. "Is that not extreme?"

"Which would you rather?" answered Caiaphas. "Should one man perish, or our whole nation? That is what's at stake. Some of his closest followers are Zealots. Could we ever hope of maintaining peace between us and the Romans if they think for even a second that there is a large-scale effort to expel them from Judea and the surrounding regions? The Zealots are foolishly obsessed with this idea."

"Would that be such a terrible thing?" asked Kish. "Do we not all want that?"

"What, do you think we'll rule with this rebel if he gains any kind of power?" asked Caiaphas. "Do you think he'll choose *us* to be part of *his* council? No. Removing our influence would be his first order of business."

"Caiaphas, the man is a homeless teacher," said Nicodemus.

"Not everyone born into humble circumstances remains in humble circumstances," the high priest replied.

"The man disrupted the temple merchants and money changers," Theophilus added. "Much was lost. His outburst was completely uncalled for. What if behavior like that becomes a habit? Or even worse, what if people join him?"

"He said he would destroy the temple," Annas said, "and in three days build it back up. He's a dangerous madman."

"Pilate would never go for this," said Ithamar. "He's the one who has to issue the decree. Pilate's advisor already told me his response to our complaints. He does not see Jesus as a threat, nor does he care about our concerns."

"You let me worry about Pilate," said Caiaphas. "Jesus claims to be Christ, a king. That's what people have reported. If that's not getting Pilate's attention, I will move him like the puppet he is. However, we have to make sure we don't arrest Jesus during the festival. It may cause another riot. Once our guards have taken him, I have no doubt the Sanhedrin will find enough evidence to condemn him."

Not all the members of the secret council were members of the Sanhedrin, but the high priest glared at the ones who were. Some nodded in agreement. But not all. Just then, a servant came into the room and said, "There's a man at the door."

"It's not a good time," said Caiaphas. "Send him away."

"He said it's urgent and can't wait. He claims to be a disciple of Jesus."

The members of the council looked at one another. Some chuckled at the timing and irony.

"This meeting has suddenly grown more interesting to me," said David, who was silent until now. "It's almost as if the Lord is granting us favor right before our very eyes."

"Send him in," said Caiaphas. "Let's see what he wants."

The man entered the room and was visibly disturbed. He twitched a bit and kept turning his head to stare into shadowy corners.

The members of the secret council looked on at this individual with disdain, as they watched him nervously move about.

"Can I help you?" asked Caiaphas. "Who are you?"

"My name is Judas Iscariot," the man said. "I've been a disciple of Jesus for the past three years. I know where he's staying. What will you give me if I deliver him to you?"

"And why would you do that?" asked Kish. "How could we trust a man breaking faith with his own group? You are obviously not trustworthy."

"My reasons are my reasons," said Judas.

"That's quite the offer, Judas," said Ithamar. "But to my friend's point, why should we believe a single thing you say?"

"You don't have to believe me," said Judas. "You'll see for yourselves when I lead you to him."

"What happened?" asked Caiaphas. "Did your master forget to feed you or something? Have you suddenly realized the futility of his mission? Are you now running out of money?"

Some of the men laughed and waited for Judas to respond. Judas twitched some more but said nothing.

"Personally, I don't care why you're doing this," said Caiaphas. "For all I know, you have finally come to your senses. Perhaps his other disciples will follow suit. Are there more traitors, or is it just you?"

Judas stared off into a shadow and said, "Just me."

"And when will you be able to do this?" asked the high priest. "In the middle of the day so that Jesus and the rest of them can ambush us? Or so all of his admirers and fellow Galileans start a riot? How do we know this isn't a trap? If you're being honest with us, we'll wait till after the festival is over and all the visitors have left. I'd be much more comfortable with that."

"That won't be necessary," said Judas. "We can do it at night. There won't be any crowds to worry about."

Caiaphas pondered the suggestion before asking his next question.

"Many of us have not seen him personally," he said. "How will we know we're arresting the right man?"

"You'll know which one to arrest when I greet him with a kiss. That will be the signal."

At hearing this, the men began to whisper to one another.

"Judas, can you please wait outside for a moment?" Annas said.

The servant escorted Judas Iscariot back into the reception hall. The door of the meeting room was then closed for privacy.

"It appears God has granted us favor, this evening," Caiaphas said. "Let's talk about this. What can go wrong?"

"It can be a trap," said Benjamin. "What if Jesus is simply using this man to start a rebellion against us? It could be a plot to murder you, Caiaphas."

"I'm not worried about that," said the high priest. "We'll bring a small army of my best soldiers."

"What if this Judas is not who he says he is?" asked Simeon. "Did he not seem strange to you? Why would Jesus keep such a deranged man so close to him?"

"I've heard Jesus befriends the sinner and even the possessed," said Solomon the scribe. "Here is a perfect example of what that has earned him."

The Council of Thirteen continued to discuss the risks of

employing Judas in their plot to arrest Jesus. Most of them were excited at the prospect and hopeful everything would work out exactly as planned. Kish even suggested they take out Lazarus, the man Jesus reportedly raised from the dead.

"Well, that should probably be done once Jesus has been taken care of," said Ithamar. "This way there won't be anyone to raise him from the dead this time."

"No one rises from the dead," said David, who happened to be a Sadducee and did not believe in the resurrection of the dead. "It was a trick."

"Trick or not," interjected Caiaphas, "the people believe it. They believe *him*."

Joseph of Arimathea remained quiet throughout this entire exchange. It became apparent Caiaphas could not be persuaded in any other direction. Joseph was no longer able to hold his tongue.

"Before an official vote is taken," he said, "I do not consent to any of this. I don't consider this a matter we should concern ourselves with."

Caiaphas glared at Joseph. The members of the council quieted down to see how this would play out.

"Is that right?" Caiaphas said. "You're still not convinced? One of Jesus's disenchanted followers has come to offer him into our hands. What does that tell you? What is your reason for this dissent?"

Joseph was not sure how to answer. Saying he didn't think Jesus committed blasphemy might be interpreted as too much of a revelation of where he stood with the man in question. Announcing to the council he did not believe Jesus had any intention of becoming a king to usurp Roman occupation could easily be used against him as well. But if he said nothing, or even worse, appeared to agree with Caiaphas, he would be directly—albeit partly—responsible for Jesus's arrest and execution. This was not something his conscience could tolerate.

"I know right from wrong," Joseph said.

Caiaphas grunted.

"Are we murderers now?" Joseph went on. "Is that what we've become? Will the Lord indeed bless our desire to rid ourselves of what annoys us?"

"If what annoys us threatens the stability of our entire nation," answered Caiaphas, "then yes, the Lord will be with us in our efforts to eradicate such wickedness from the land."

"And yet, you wouldn't dare raise an army to confront our true oppressors. You'd rather keep the peace at all costs, even if it means sentencing an innocent man to death. Or have we all forgotten the Lord hates punishing the innocent?"

"Innocent," Caiaphas repeated. "That's an interesting word, Joseph. I'm beginning to wonder if you, yourself, have become one of his secret followers."

"I don't appreciate accusations. I accepted your invitation to this council as a privilege to assist the high priest in his most important decisions. It's been my honor. But if those decisions are no more than schemes to condemn men who threaten your influence over the people and who are guilty of no more than teaching and healing on the Sabbath or—in the case of Lazarus—raising people from the dead, then I will have no part in it. I officially resign from this council."

Joseph rose from his seat.

"Are you sure you want to do this?" asked Caiaphas. "I can make things very uncomfortable—" Annas then squeezed his son-in-law's arm to stop him from finishing that sentence.

"Thank you for sharing your thoughts, Joseph," said Annas. "You may go now."

Annas then whispered to Caiaphas, "No one contributes more to the temple treasury than Joseph. Be mindful of your dealings with such valuable men."

Joseph stared at Judas Iscariot on his way out and said, "Your greed is about to call down a curse upon your life, Judas. I'd leave right now if I were you. Have nothing to do with this wickedness."

Judas snarled. This made Joseph recoil as if a dog was about to bite him.

When Joseph exited the home of Caiaphas, he immediately went to warn Jesus of the plot against him.

Caiaphas did not respond to his father-in-law's admonishment. Instead, he addressed the rest of the council.

"Does anyone else object to what we're trying to accomplish tonight?" he asked. "Does anyone wish to follow Joseph? Now is your time."

Nicodemus squirmed in his seat for a bit. He was astounded at his friend's boldness. Never could he dream of speaking so forthrightly to the high priest. He managed to muster enough courage to rise from his seat as well.

"You too, Nicodemus?" asked Caiaphas.

"I...I," he stuttered. "I'm not sure."

"Not sure," Caiaphas repeated. "I do recall you questioning our stance on Jesus when the temple guards gave their report. Has the man put you in a trance too? Perhaps you need to examine where your allegiance lies. You're either for us or against us. But I should remind you, that if you walk out now, you will be officially and permanently off this council."

Annas squeezed his son-in-law's arm again. He wanted to remind Caiaphas how much wealth Nicodemus possessed. But Caiaphas moved his arm away. His father-in-law was beginning to annoy him.

Nicodemus felt everyone staring at him, waiting for a response. He remembered Jesus's words when he visited him in secret one night. Jesus told him unless one is born again he cannot see the kingdom of God. This saying consumed Nicodemus ever since. He suddenly imagined himself in a type of womb. Light was breaking through a crack in the darkness of his spirit. Boldness stirred in the depths of his soul, along with it a determination to emerge from the darkness and into that light.

"I mean no disrespect," Nicodemus said. "I resign from this council."

"You may go," Annas told him.

Nicodemus said nothing to Judas on his way out. He stepped into the cool night air and breathed in a freedom he never knew existed. He looked up at the stars and whispered a prayer of gratitude to the Lord. It would be a long time before he could articulate what took place that night. All he knew was that he was a new man.

"We'll have to watch those two," Caiaphas said. "Anyone else have something to say?"

The council remained quiet. Most did not want to jeopardize their position or relationship with the high priest, as it afforded certain privileges.

"Very well. Let's get on with this."

A vote was then taken anonymously. Caiaphas was angered when he saw that not everyone consented to the plan. He wished he knew who the other dissenters were besides Joseph and

Nicodemus. But more than half of the remaining eleven council members decided Jesus needed to be taken care of permanently. And now Caiaphas had what he needed: someone close to Jesus willing to betray him.

Judas Iscariot was brought back in. The council offered him thirty pieces of silver, which they felt fair, even generous. He was to be paid as soon as Jesus was in their custody. Judas agreed to these terms. They then decided on which night this would take place.

When the meeting finished and everyone went home, Caiaphas and his father-in-law remained talking at the table.

"Pilate will be a problem," Annas said. "Too many people admire Jesus. How many *loyals* would you say we have?"

"At least five hundred men, all city residents," Caiaphas answered. "That's not including their families. Loyals throughout Judea are here for the festival as well. Hundreds, I'm sure."

"We'll need witnesses to build our case and a crowd to pressure Pilate," Annas said. "If we organize this right, we should have well over a thousand, maybe even two thousand. That should be enough. Get your messengers ready. I'll do the same. Send word to our loyals first thing tomorrow."

Seek and Find

Simon arose early in the morning as usual. Dinah tried her best to talk her husband out of it. But as Caleb so clearly stated, his brother had always been an *all-or-nothing* kind of man. There was no stopping him once he put his mind to something.

Simon decided to put his twins' sense of adventure to good use. They were to help him search for Jesus of Nazareth. There were rumors of his whereabouts. Some say he was staying in Jericho as a guest of Zacchaeus the tax collector. Others said he was somewhere in Bethany. This was close enough to send the twins to investigate. However, Simon was confident he'd find him if he walked the streets of Jerusalem.

He spent much of his time interviewing random people to see what he could find out. No one seemed to know where Jesus was, but several told stories about their encounters with him.

He met a man from Galilee who claimed Jesus healed him of leprosy. Another from Capernaum said he was paralyzed until he met Jesus. Simon was told tales of demons and sicknesses being driven out of people, even entire crowds being miraculously fed. They can't all be lies, he thought. How can so many people be wrong?

He approached a poor elderly woman begging on a corner. Simon offered her a silver coin in exchange for any clue of where he could find Jesus.

"This is hardly worth the silver," she said. "But I thank you for your generosity. He's in the temple courts, teaching right now." Simon was astonished. He didn't imagine Jesus would show his face there again after the commotion he caused the day before. He gave the woman two silver coins and ran to the temple to see for himself.

Sure enough, there was Jesus, standing before a captivated audience hanging on to his every word. Simon tried his best to work his way to the front, but people were not letting him through. The crowd only grew thicker the closer he got to Jesus, so he stayed somewhere in the middle.

One of the Herodians in the crowd asked, "What's your opinion, should we pay taxes to Caesar or not?" Simon thought the inquiry to be strange. Why would anyone ask a religious figure such a political thing? Jesus rebuked the man almost immediately for trying to trap him and requested to see a coin used to pay taxes. He asked the Herodian to tell him whose portrait was on the coin. The man said, "Caesar's." Jesus then replied, "Give to Caesar what is Caesar's and to God what is God's."

This answer stunned Simon, but he wasn't quite sure why. Perhaps it was the clear demarcation between the things of God and the things of man. Jesus was not promoting any kind of rebellion against the Romans as Caleb suspected. He's even encouraging Jews to pay their taxes!

The Herodians, along with many Pharisees, left the crowd. Simon was finally able to maneuver his way to the front.

Jesus continued to teach. He spoke of Moses, Abraham, marriage, and resurrection. One man asked which was the greatest commandment. Simon and just about everyone in the crowd leaned in to hear Jesus answer, not wanting to miss a single word. Jesus proclaimed in a loud voice as if wanting the entire city to hear, "Listen up all of Israel: The Lord our God. The Lord is one. Love the Lord your God with all your heart, soul, mind, and strength. The second greatest commandment is very similar. Love your neighbor as yourself. There is no commandment greater than these two."

Now why on earth would Jesus say such a thing? Simon wondered. How could you compare loving God with loving your fellow man? Simon knew he'd ponder these things for years to come. Those in the crowd still trying to test Jesus were silenced. Many more left at this point. When much of the crowd had dispersed, Simon wanted to approach Jesus but felt dwarfed by his wisdom. Though Simon had made up his mind to follow Jesus, he had not yet sold his possessions and given his money to the poor, which Jesus had instructed him to do. And so he felt inadequate to say anything. Instead, he quietly fell back and followed behind to see what Jesus would do and say next.

Jesus went to where many wealthy people formed a line to put money in the temple treasury. Immediately, Simon jumped at the chance to offer a small pouch of gold coins, hoping Jesus would notice. He then ran right behind to where Jesus's twelve disciples were sitting, along with a few others, now hoping to blend in.

Jesus pointed out a poor widow who finally made her way to the front of the offering line. It was Micah's mother, Hannah. She gave only two small copper coins. Jesus said, "I speak the truth when I tell you this woman has given more than everyone else today. The rest gave out of their abundance, but those two small copper coins were all this poor widow had to live on."

Simon almost had a heart attack when he heard this. He jumped to his feet.

"Simon, my friend," said Jesus with a big smile.

He remembers me, thought Simon, but he had no idea what to say or do next.

"Rabbi," he responded sheepishly, then took off running.

A Story About Kezia

Having the day off due to his *monstrosity of a face*—as Pilate so eloquently put it—along with his utter exhaustion, Longinus awoke late in the afternoon. He sat up and only remembered he had one eye when he couldn't open both of them. His pain was in full bloom, and he felt his face had swollen even more on that side. His son was sitting in a chair staring at him as if he had been waiting for hours for his father to wake up, wondering if he would at all.

"Did you eat something?" Longinus asked the boy.

"Some fruit and bread," he answered. "Does it hurt?"

"What, my scratch? Come here. Let me show you something."

The boy rose to his feet and walked over to his father. Longinus gently tickled his son's face.

"It feels a bit like this," he said.

The young Longinus laughed and said, "I don't believe you."

"Are you calling your father a liar?"

"No," he said promptly. "I just don't believe you."

"Good," his father said. "You're young. Yet, you recognize a crazy statement when you hear one. When you've lived as long as I have, you'll realize most of the crazy statements people make are untrue."

The boy thought about this, as his father went to get something to eat from the table.

"Abba?"

"Yes?"

"Have you heard of Jesus of Nazareth?"

His father grunted as he tore into some apples and dates.

"Have you met him?" his son asked.

"In a meeting yesterday, I heard about some commotion he started at the temple. But no, I haven't met him."

"I've heard things about him. Crazy things."

"So have I. People healed of various diseases and so forth. But what did I tell you about crazy statements people make?"

"That they're probably untrue."

"Exactly. Nonsense. That's all. People believe what they want to believe, son."

"But what if they *are* true? I heard one man was even raised from the dead."

Longinus chuckled to himself but did not want to embarrass his son. He faced the boy and put a hand on his shoulder.

"The dead don't rise. Your mother is gone. I wish that weren't true. Maybe even more than you."

His son looked down in defeat.

"Look at me," Longinus said.

He begrudgingly looked up. Longinus took the boy's right hand and placed it on his heart.

"This is where she will never die. You understand?"

The boy nodded and fought back tears.

"You keep her alive in here," he went on. "As will I. Memories are eternal. So we must never forget."

The boy wrapped his arms around his father. Longinus was not used to such tenderness, as he spent most of his time in Caesarea and would only see Kezia and the boy during religious festivals when Pilate would travel with large cohorts of soldiers. His days were generally filled with training men to be harder than rocks, both inside and out. Just three weeks prior, Longinus was demonstrating to a small unit how to properly take a punch to the gut. He ruptured the spleen of the unfortunate soldier who bravely —or foolishly—volunteered to take such a severe hit to the stomach. Nearly killed him. Now Longinus felt a mixture of extreme gratitude and fear. He returned his son's embrace but wondered if he had done the right thing not leaving him with Nathan.

After a while, the young Longinus said, "You know, Mother met Jesus one time."

"Really? Did he perform any miracle or trick for her?"

"No, but he did save her life. A bunch of men wanted to kill her."

Longinus looked at the boy's face with his one good eye.

"What do you mean?" he said. "When was this? Why would anyone try to kill your mother?"

"Mother didn't tell me. But I heard her talking about it with Nathan the night it happened. They thought I was asleep."

"And what did you hear?" Longinus asked.

"I don't want to tell you."

"Son, you're with *me* now. I promise there is no trouble coming for you. Nathan isn't here. Your mother isn't here. It's just us. You have nothing to worry about. I want to know."

"Promise you won't feel bad about it," the boy said.

"Look at me when I speak."

The boy looked at his father's face, half of it still covered with strips of blood-stained linen.

"I lost your mother and an eye in the same hour. I have enough to feel bad about, believe me. So tell me."

The boy took a deep breath and reluctantly confessed, "I heard her say something about men catching her in bed with a married man in the city."

The boy looked at his father for a reaction. But his father of course knew more of Kezia's profession than he and simply asked, "And then what happened?"

"Well," the boy went on. "She told Nathan that the mean men dragged her out of bed and out of the man's home. She was almost naked and they brought her to Jesus. They wanted to throw rocks at her and asked what Jesus thought."

"And what did Jesus say?"

"Jesus said that anyone who had no sins could throw the first stone. The men dropped their rocks and went away."

"Clever," said Longinus. "Is that all?"

"The last thing I remember before I fell asleep was Mother telling Nathan that Jesus did not condemn her."

"Condemn her? What authority does Jesus have to condemn or not condemn anyone? That doesn't matter, does it? I should thank this man for saving her. It was more than I was able to do." Now it was time for the elder Longinus to look down in defeat. But his shame was promptly interrupted by a knock at the door. It was the physician.

"Let's have a look at that eye," he said when the door was opened.

The next few minutes were physically painful for Longinus and emotionally painful for his son to watch. But they both got through it. The doctor reapplied some ointment to the wound and left.

Longinus got dressed in full centurion garb.

"But Abba," the boy said. "I thought you didn't have to work today."

"People get out of my way when I wear this. You'll see. Now let's go find Jesus of Nazareth. We both owe him our gratitude."

Rats

There was no telling whether it was day or night in the pit. There were no windows. It was always dark, illuminated by only two oil lamps hanging from wall-mounted hooks. The guards often allowed the light to go out and then refused to replenish the oil or replace the wick for hours, leaving the prisoners in complete darkness. No one ever got used to the unbearable stench. There was no choice but to live with it. The guards did their best to keep their distance from the pit where the prisoners were held. They were close enough to hear them call, but far enough to tolerate the smell better.

"I wonder if she's already packed her things," Micah said. "I wonder where she'll go."

"Who?" Barabbas asked.

"Who do you think?" asked Ehud. "His mommy. She's all our baby friend can speak of for some reason. I thought he was a man. I truly did. We've robbed people together. Killed when necessary. He served as an Upper City watchman. Yet, here he is going on and on about his mother. Be a man already! You've made your choices in life, now deal with them!"

"Leave him alone," said Barabbas. "We're all in the pit, are we not? What difference does it make how any of us spend our final hours? Let him be. Honoring your parents is a commandment."

"Oh, shut up!" said Ehud. Then a rat bit him. "Shoo!" he shouted. Ehud kicked it and yelled, "Get away from me!"

That same rat, along with five others, found a dead prisoner and began gnawing at various parts of his body. Several more rats found their way to the prisoner.

"Guards!" Ehud shouted over and over.

A minute or two passed before a prison guard finally came to the locked door and stood there. He covered his nose but did not open the door.

"Please," Ehud continued. "You have to remove this dead prisoner. We can't take the rats!"

"Is that an order?" the guard asked jokingly. He laughed quietly to himself and walked back to his post. Ehud shouted all the more but to no avail.

Felix had a fever and floated in and out of consciousness. Shaking and drenched with sweat, he'd awake to the sight of rats consuming the dead prisoner and wondered when he was next.

Micah drifted off to sleep and dreamed of his mother in a castle. He didn't think she had enough gold to afford one. But he liked imagining his mother well taken care of. In this fantasy, there was a table full of food. Micah found himself in the dream as well. He was married to a beautiful woman and had five children running around their garden. His mother was chasing them and laughing. He was woken up abruptly by Ehud shouting at him, "Take that stupid smile off your face, Micah!"

Divi Filius

The young Longinus noticed his father was quite right. People got out of their way as soon as they saw the centurion of such great stature.

"How will we know where Jesus is?" the boy asked.

"Since he likes to stir up trouble at the temple, let's start there."

When they approached the complex, Simon came running out of an area called the Court of the Women, which is where the temple treasury was located. He bumped right into Longinus. It was a bit like running into a human wall. Simon found himself on the ground instantly, dumbfounded.

"Watch where you're going?" Longinus reprimanded.

Simon stared at the tree of a man standing over him, blocking out the sun. When he realized it was a centurion, a wave of fear washed over him.

"I'm...I'm quite sorry. Forgive my manners. I'll be on my way." Simon stood to his feet, dusted himself off, and continued running.

The boy stared at the strange man who had the nerve to carelessly run into his father. A bit disappointed, he said, "Abba, I thought maybe you'd punch him in the face or something."

"I'm not in the mood, son."

The boy pointed to a crowd gathered inside the court. He and his father went to investigate. Many women and men were gathered near the temple treasury, listening to a man speak. Longinus and his son walked closer to the crowd.

"Who is that?" Longinus asked a man leaning against a pillar.

Startled by the huge centurion speaking in his native Aramaic, the man answered, "That's Jesus of Nazareth, a teacher. Some say he's the Son of God. He's prophesying right now."

Son of God? Longinus thought. He was familiar with the Latin version of the term—Divi filius—sometimes assigned to Roman emperors. This was startling enough, but Longinus was more shocked by what Jesus had to say.

"Nation will rise against nation, and kingdom against kingdom." Jesus spoke of famines and earthquakes, pestilences, and signs from the heavens. He spoke of his followers being brought before kings and governors and being thrown into prison and put to death.

Maybe Pilate *should* be worried, Longinus thought. He listened to the rest of the strange sermon, not wanting to interrupt. When Jesus finished, the crowd dispersed except for his disciples and some of their wives and children.

Longinus and his son walked up to Jesus and stood before him.

Jesus smiled at the boy and looked up at the large centurion. His disciples cowered at the sight of the enormous Roman general.

"What can I do for you?" asked Jesus.

The boy eagerly tugged on his father's arm to whisper in his ear, "Tell him to heal your eye."

"You can't do anything for me," Longinus answered. "I've only come to thank you."

"Thank me?"

"Yes, you saved my wife's life."

"Mother was not your wife," the boy interjected. "Was she?" Longinus glared down at his son. The boy understood he was to be quiet.

"The woman I loved," Longinus went on. "It's my understanding you saved her from being stoned. I want to thank you for that."

Jesus remembered exactly who he was referring to and felt compassion for Longinus and his son.

"Life is spared one day," Jesus said, "to be taken on another. But whoever believes in me will have eternal life."

"If you say so," Longinus said. "I won't forget your kind act. Please accept my gratitude."

Jesus nodded and said, "Is that all?"

The frustrated boy pointed to his own eye to remind his father to ask for a healing.

Jesus laughed in amusement and said, "Your boy has great faith!"

"Yes," Longinus said. "It's unfortunate. I'm working on ridding him of such nonsense. Enjoy the rest of your day."

Longinus and his son turned to head back to the governor's palace.

"Abba, wait a minute," his son said, looking back at Jesus. "Let's not leave yet." But Longinus grabbed the boy by his arm to exit the temple courts.

"Why didn't you ask him to heal your eye?" his son asked. He could've done it right then and there."

Longinus stopped walking to face the boy and said, "No, he couldn't have, son. Those are just stories. Lies. He's a good man. I can tell that much. Certainly brave enough to stop a mob from killing your mother. But he's no magician. He's clever with words. That's all. We thanked him for his kindness. It's important to thank people when they've done something extraordinarily kind. That doesn't mean we need to believe in every crazy thing they tell us. Understand?"

The boy sighed in frustration and nodded. When they resumed their walk, he muttered loud enough for his father to hear, "It wouldn't have hurt you to ask for a healing." Longinus ignored the remark. The boy kicked rocks along the way.

Blessing vs the Blesser

Caleb sat quietly as he ate that evening. He listened to the twins recount their unsuccessful search for Jesus in Bethany. They had gotten back much later than Simon and were excited to tell their tale. They hadn't found who they were looking for but did manage to find some trouble. They accidentally knocked over a cart of fruit and spilled all of the contents onto the ground. The merchant chased them through the streets, forcing the boys to split up. It took nearly two hours before they found each other again. Joanna in particular found her brothers amusing. If they weren't making her scream and tell on them, they were making her laugh. Dinah's heart filled with joy to see her only daughter laughing after such a traumatic ordeal the other night. Perhaps that was the very reason the rest of the family laughed as well. All except Caleb, who refused to engage.

"You did not find him," Simon said, "because I did. He was teaching in the temple courts. I suspect he'll be there every day till the festival is over. I think he and his disciples will stay in town."

"Did you speak to him?" the twins asked, anxiously.

"Yes and no. I didn't want to interrupt. He's a very wise man. The people were captivated by his every word. I'm going back to hear him again tomorrow. Hopefully he'll be there. Would anyone like to join me?"

"So you're one of his disciples now," Caleb said, as he sipped his wine. The sudden sound of Caleb's voice silenced the table almost instantly. Joanna was young but old enough to recognize an awkward moment. "Soon you'll make your financial ruin complete," he went on. "That's what you said, right? Well, you won't drag me down with you. No. I won't let that happen. Is it not written, 'But remember the Lord your God, for it is he who gives you the power to get wealth'? Therefore, wealth is a blessing, not a curse. Is it not? So you will have to go down all by yourself, brother. You want to die empty-handed? Be my guest."

"Caleb, not now," Leah said. But Caleb simply raised his hand, requesting she not get involved.

"We all die empty-handed," said Simon. "And I can quote scripture too, brother. How about this one? 'Naked I came from my mother's womb, and naked shall I return.'"

Caleb stared at Simon with contempt in his eyes. He grunted and got up from the table, leaving the family alone to bask in the tension that hung in the air like an impenetrable fog.

No one spoke for a few minutes after this. They all quietly finished their meals. One by one, Leah and the children left the table leaving Simon and Dinah to talk.

"So what is the plan?" Dinah asked her husband.

"The plan?"

"Yes, Simon. The plan. You haven't been able to stop talking about your encounter with Jesus since it happened. It's like you're stuck. Is Caleb right? Do you truly want to become another one of this man's disciples? Where would that leave us? Destitute and poor? Is that the Lord's will for us? So yes, I want to know your plan for your family. Please tell me."

Simon sighed in frustration and thought about how to articulate his thoughts.

"I don't know, Dinah," he said. "I don't have a plan at the moment. Is not the Lord our provider? Do you think I have the power to do anything apart from his will? What can I accomplish without the blessing of God?"

"Exactly! So why would you throw away what God has already blessed you with? Is that not foolishly testing the Lord? People see our riches and immediately know we are favored by God. Why are you suddenly questioning it?"

"I haven't thrown anything away."

"Not yet, but that is what he told you to do when you first met him? Isn't that right? Did he not tell you to sell your possessions and give all the earnings to the poor?"

"He did."

"Haven't you already announced to us all your plans to do just that?"

"I have."

"You're already going after him. Listening to his teachings. Sending our sons to look for him. So is your brother right, will you soon make our financial ruin complete?"

Simon thought about the question for a moment before giving his response.

"I don't know, Dinah. All I know is that I'm the one being tested. Not God. Are we to love the blessing more than the blesser?" His wife did not answer, though she did stare at him with the same contempt he saw in his brother's eyes. He went on regardless. "Dinah, when I listen to Jesus speak, life flows through me. I'm filled with hope and possibility. Our wealth has been great. I don't question that. It *has* been a blessing. But Jesus was right. I've placed my trust in wealth more than God. I've erected it as an idol and worshipped at its altar. I bow down to it. I serve it. I can see that now. I want to learn a new way to live."

"You want to learn how to beg," said Dinah. "Keep going and you will get there. I just wish I didn't have to join you."

"Have faith, Dinah. Trust the Lord."

His wife said nothing.

"Why don't you come with me tomorrow?" he added.

"Come with you? Where?"

"To listen to Jesus speak."

"Oh, I don't know," she said. She stood to her feet at this point. "I have to help Leah with the food preparation. There's lots to do around here. I'm getting tired just thinking about it."

"It doesn't have to be all day. But I want you to hear for yourself."

Dinah looked at her husband. She saw the sincerity in his eyes and it frightened her.

"Fine," she answered. "I'll go. But only for a little while. I make no promises to like the man or agree with anything he says."

This made Simon smile. It was enough that Dinah had agreed to come with him. She'd see for herself whether or not Jesus of Nazareth was a lunatic, making everyone who listened to him just as crazy.

The next morning, they arose. Simon was trying to recall his dream from the previous night. He distinctly remembered the image of a leather bag full of gold coins. More and more of the dream came back to him as he concentrated. Simon then recalled turning the leather bag upside down to empty it. When coins stopped falling out, he reached in to ensure it was empty. Yet he discovered more coins. He removed them and turned the leather bag upside down a second time. More gold came pouring out. The bag finally emptied, or so he thought. He reached in to check. The same thing happened all over again. It seemed impossible for the leather bag to run out of gold coins. Simon thought about the dream for a while. Then it was time to go. The children went off to play in the garden. Caleb went about his work, getting the spice carts ready for deliveries.

"Where are you two going?" Leah asked Simon and Dinah, as they were leaving the home.

"Please don't ask me that," Dinah said.

"We're going to listen to Jesus speak," said Simon. "Would you like to come?"

Leah chuckled at the notion and said, "Caleb would kill me, I think. Or perhaps collapse dead, himself. He's had enough trouble this week. I won't tell him where you're going."

"Doesn't matter, Leah. We'll be home before evening."

Simon and Dinah headed off to the temple courts. The crowd had already gathered. It was much larger than the previous day.

"My goodness, there are a lot of people here," Dinah said. "Is that him?" She pointed to Jesus, who was already speaking in a loud voice so all could hear.

"That's him," said Simon. They squeezed and pushed themselves through the thick crowd and fought their way to the middle of it to find a seat on the ground.

Jesus said, "Whoever believes in me does not believe in me only, but also in the one who sent me. If you see me, you see who sent me as well."

"Isn't that blasphemy," Dinah whispered to her husband.

"Just listen. Make judgments later."

Jesus went on and spoke about how he came into the world as a light and how whoever believes and follows him should not remain in darkness. Dinah wanted with everything in her to not believe. She wanted evidence she could slap her husband's face with. She wished to say, "See, what did I tell you? He's a complete and utter lunatic." But the more Jesus spoke, the more his words burned within her. She felt a fire rise inside her she didn't know existed. It was a mix of hope and conviction. Jesus spoke of many things that morning. Sin, worship, caring for others, and money as a master. It was the last point that broke Dinah down. She finally understood what Simon was talking about and recognized the chains she was shackled to. She also felt a freedom coursing through her that had the power to break those chains.

When Jesus finished speaking, Simon turned to his wife to find her crying.

"What's wrong?" he asked.

"Everything," she answered. She wiped away her tears. "Our end has come. You were right."

Simon laughed at the statement and said. "My love, I have a feeling this is only the beginning of a great adventure. Let's leave, shall we?"

Hope for the Hopeless

Marcus arose earlier than usual the following morning to check in on Felix before his daily work responsibilities began. He brought the doctor with him once more.

"I think you should let your friend be?" the doctor said, before reaching the inner cell of the pit.

"And *I* think you should hold your tongue unless I ask you a question. Another two days have gone by, and—once again—you are nearly impossible to find. If he's dead, I'm holding *you* directly responsible."

The doctor said nothing to this, nor would he ever admit to hiding around corners whenever he saw Marcus.

One of the prison guards let them in. Felix was not better. He was sweating, shaking, and in a state of delirium. There was vomit on his chest and the ground near him. He answered with either yes-or-no nods or shakes of the head, but not with words.

"There, there, let's take a look," the doctor said. Despite the treatment from their previous visit, Felix's wound was still infected and getting worse.

A bit frightened of a beating from Marcus, the physician was apprehensive to share bad news. But it was his job. He mustered up the courage and braced himself. "I don't think I can do anything," he said. He showed Marcus the wound so it would be self-explanatory. It was. Marcus, however, wanted Felix to be strong enough for the escape. He had no intention of carrying his enormous friend. There was no hiding such a large Roman decurion. If Felix couldn't walk properly and look like he was on duty, Marcus doubted his plan would work.

"But you will try," said Marcus.

"Excuse me," said Ehud, who watched this entire interaction, though he couldn't quite hear the whispers. Marcus turned toward Ehud.

"Why is that man getting special treatment? We are *all* suffering in here."

Marcus walked over to Ehud and stood in front of him, staring into his eyes. Ehud regretted his words immediately. Even before Marcus punched him in the stomach.

"We will treat who we will treat," Marcus said. "Is that clear?"

Ehud nodded and did his best to catch his breath. The other prisoners stayed quiet. Marcus then whispered to Felix an encouragement to stay alive. He would soon be out of the pit and healing somewhere pleasant, without flesh-consuming rats, and with better food and no horrific stench.

When Marcus and the doctor left, Barabbas turned his head toward Ehud and asked, "Are you alright?"

"Leave me alone." Ehud was still catching his breath.

"Relax. It was only a question. You shouldn't have said anything."

"Should I be a coward?" said Ehud. "What do I have to lose by speaking my piece? Can it get any worse?"

"Well, you wouldn't have gotten punched. I can say that much."

Ehud could not argue with this.

Turning his attention toward Felix, Barabbas asked, "I assume you're one of the traitors? I only knew of Silvanus but was told there were others. You must be one of them. Why else would they spend so much time with you? Thank you. Please accept my sincerest gratitude. I know it's not easy to betray your own. But it was the right thing to do. Oppression needs friends in various places if it is to be overcome."

Felix lifted his head to see Barabbas. With great effort, he managed to get out, "Freedom is not free."

"Indeed, not," said Barabbas. "We're all paying the cost, right now."

"We were ripped off," added Ehud, as he did his best to speak through discomfort and pain.

"Interesting commentary," said Barabbas, "coming from someone who abandoned post before the mission was even complete."

"What can I say?" said Ehud. "I know a bad deal when I see it."

"We all have to pay the same price." This time it was Micah who had finally joined the conversation. Barabbas and Ehud had gotten used to Micah's silence after he had finally stopped talking about his mother.

"What is that supposed to mean?" asked Ehud.

"Whether we fight for justice, live selfishly, mind our own business, become rich or poor—death comes for us all, does it not?"

"You know," said Ehud, "I think I liked you better when you were whining about your mommy."

"This is true, Micah," said Barabbas. "But I want the Lord to be able to look at my life and see that I stood up for what's right."

"Well," said Ehud. "You better hope the Lord sees things your way. I gave up on that a long time ago."

In a broken and strained voice, Felix said, "A new kingdom is coming, my friends. Peace will one day rule."

Barabbas did not respond but felt both compassion and admiration for this Roman who shared his fate.

"Can someone tell me what this man is talking about?" asked Ehud. "Peace is not in sight. It's not even on the horizon."

"He's talking about hope," said Micah.

"You're one to talk," said Ehud. *"Death is coming for us all. Nothing matters."*

"Both of you, shut up," said Barabbas. Then turning to Felix, he said, "Thank you for your kind words." But Felix had already fallen asleep.

Passover

Jerusalem was bustling about with Passover preparation. There were last-minute marketplace runs, countless lambs being slain, families gathering at various homes, and Roman soldiers patrolling the streets.

Back in his father's room in the barracks, the young Longinus looked at the table of bread and fruit in disappointment. His father noticed this and asked what was wrong.

"We're not ready for Passover," the boy answered. "That isn't unleavened bread at the table. There's no lamb. No bitter herbs. We'll need four cups of wine. We have nothing. Who will tell the story of our deliverance from Egypt? We need to pray and sing the Hallel."

"Son, I don't celebrate that," his father said. "You know that. And as you can see, there's plenty of wine. I can easily get roasted meat for us. There's no shortage of anything in the palace. I'm hungry, myself."

"Not the same. I always went with Dod—I mean Nathan—to choose our lamb. We also have to remove any leaven in the room. I can teach you all the things we need to do if you want."

The mention of Nathan annoyed Longinus. At that particular moment, it wasn't anything about the innkeeper's faults that bothered him. Rather, it was the image of them operating as a family without him. Longinus wanted to choose his words carefully but be as honest as possible.

"We have different gods," he said. "I pray to Jupiter, Juno, Mars, and Minerva, among others. I'll teach you about them sometime. I have my own rituals." As soon as the words left his mouth, he remembered pledging to follow Kezia's god if she came with him. Now that she was gone, he wasn't sure if he was bound by this oath.

"But it's Passover," his son protested. "We do this every year."

Longinus saw the long road ahead of him. Raising his son would be riddled with difficulty. The boy already had his god and traditions. Longinus wasn't sure he believed in his Roman gods, but he prayed to them nonetheless. Usually for protection. He reasoned they must be listening to him, for he was still alive. Countless fights, battles, and skirmishes. Many brushes with death, but none strong enough to take him.

"We'll speak more of this when I return," Longinus said. "I'll be on duty today. Stay in the room and bar the door."

"Wait," the boy said.

"Yes?"

"Take all this unleavened bread with you. It shouldn't be in the room."

Later that day, Dinah and Leah spoke to their husbands about keeping peace in the home during Passover, especially during the meal. The men grunted in agreement and mostly kept to themselves. They went through the ritualistic motions and did their best to pretend their minds were not preoccupied.

The first cup of wine was poured. Caleb recited scripture, "I am the Lord, and I will bring you out from under the yoke of the Egyptians."

With each cup, Simon and Dinah both thought about their love of money. The Lord was about to bring them out of this slavery and deliver them from bondage. They now needed to trust God would redeem them and take them as his people. Wealth would no longer be their Pharaoh. Though neither uttered any of these private thoughts aloud.

While on duty, Longinus asked around and managed to purchase a few items needed for the Passover meal. After he finished his shift, he brought back to the room roasted lamb, bitter herbs, and unleavened bread. The boy was delighted. Longinus let his son lead the Passover meal ritual. He repeated various scriptures as the boy instructed, though he did not sing. Longinus also drank far more than four cups of wine.

Rebel

Well before dawn the following morning, a rooster crowed and woke Pontius Pilate. He had already settled it in his mind the night before to get going with trials and executions so he didn't have to remain in Jerusalem any longer than planned. Inside the palace, in the large front atrium, there was a section for questioning criminals and hearing testimony. Pilate took his seat and called in various generals and officials. Longinus and Marcus were among them.

"I'd like to start trials today," he said. Pilate's thoughts were disrupted when he took notice of Longinus. He called the centurion forward.

"Take that ridiculous head wrapping off. You look like you're about to die. Are you? I should know."

"No, sir," Longinus answered. He unwrapped the linen and removed the poultice. Pilate had a servant discard it at once. Then he stood up and walked over to examine the wound.

"Still positively disgusting," the governor observed. "Does it hurt?"

"No," Longinus lied.

"Well, if that doesn't scare off my foes, I don't know what will. It's a shame your helmet will cover most of it. You're not bleeding anymore. Go back to your place now." Longinus did so and Pilate took his seat again.

"I don't want to stay in this city longer than necessary," he continued. "Let's execute whoever we have to and make these trials quick and painless...Well, quick, anyway—Oh, what is it now?" Pilate saw through the open entrance of the Praetorium an angry crowd marching toward him. Longinus and Marcus looked at one another. The mob of loyals was being led by Caiaphas, members of the Sanhedrin, and the Council of Thirteen. Joseph and Nicodemus had already been replaced. Some members of the secret council refused to participate. The high priest and his father-in-law took note. Temple guards were holding a man that Longinus recognized immediately when they were close enough to see with his one good eye. The man was Jesus of Nazareth.

"Just one trip," Pilate said. "That's all I ask for. Just one trip to this awful city where I don't have to deal with such lunacy. Is that too much to ask? They must've brought the entire Sanhedrin with them. Who are all these people?" The crowd gathered around the Stone Pavement where the governor's judgments were pronounced, but they did not enter the palace. Pilate instructed one of his advisors to go outside and see what they wanted. He motioned for Longinus and another centurion to accompany him.

The three of them exited the palace and met the crowd of angry men that seemed to be getting larger by the second. Longinus stared coldly into the eyes of the temple guards who held and led Jesus, bound tightly with rope. He noticed one of the guards seemed deeply troubled. Shocked even. There was dried blood that started from one of this man's ears and ran down the side of his face and neck. Longinus then looked at Jesus who had a black and swollen eye and a fat bloodied lip. He wondered about the struggle that took place.

It was obvious that Caiaphas was leading this ordeal, and so it was he whom Pilate's advisor addressed when he said, "The governor would like to know your request before you approach."

Caiaphas answered without hesitation, "This man is subverting our nation and leading many people to rebel against Roman authority. He claims to be Christ, a king. We cannot enter the palace. It will defile us."

Leaving Longinus and the other centurion, the advisor returned to give the message to Pilate.

"A king?" Pilate asked, with slight amusement. He stared curiously at their captive through the entrance. "He doesn't look very kingly, does he?"

"No sir," his advisor answered.

"Very well, let them approach. But I don't want the whole crowd coming. Four at the most."

"Sir," the advisor said. "They won't enter the palace, for it will make them ceremonially unclean. Passover is not finished. They request you come out and talk with them."

Pilate sighed and cursed under his breath. He stood up and went to meet the men outside. An entourage surrounded him as he walked.

"Caiaphas, old friend," Pilate began. "Why do you bother me so early in the morning? What charges do you bring against this man?"

"If he weren't a criminal," Caiaphas said, "would we have brought him to you?"

"I have a prison full of insurrectionists, several days of trials to get through, and a minor headache. Why don't you judge him according to your own law and leave me alone? Go. Enjoy your holy day."

Jonathan, son of Annas, spoke up, "Governor, we don't have the authority to execute anyone. You know that."

"Execute? For what reason does this man need to be executed?"

"Allow me to list his offenses," said Theophilus, Jonathan's brother. "This man is subverting our nation. He organized the insurrection and will lead more if we let him live. He even opposes taxes to Caesar and claims to be Christ, a king."

"You know who else hates paying taxes?" Pilate asked. They all looked at one another, wondering if they were supposed to answer. "Everyone." Then looking at Jesus, Pilate asked, "So, your majesty, is it true? Should we all bow down to you? Are you the king of the Jews?"

Jesus looked into Pilate's eyes and said, "It is as you say."

The religious leaders went into an uproar after this. They went on and on with their list of offenses, hoping one of them would get the attention of the governor. Pilate was not convinced Jesus had led the insurrection. In fact, Pilate wasn't convinced Jesus was guilty of anything more than annoying Jerusalem's religious elite, which pleased him very much. He told them he found no basis for a charge against Jesus, certainly not one worthy of execution. After hearing all the trouble the Nazarene had been stirring throughout Judea, starting from Galilee, Pilate interrupted them.

"Wait a minute," he said. "Stop talking for two seconds, please! He's from Nazareth, you say? So he's a Galilean?"

"He is," they replied.

"Well, why didn't you say that in the first place? This man is not my problem. Galilee is Herod's jurisdiction. Not mine. You should know that, Caiaphas. Bring your case to Herod. Let *him* deal with it."

Pilate sent two centurions to lead Jesus and his accusers to Herod's nearby residence. He then went back inside the palace and sat in his chair.

Turning to all the generals and officials present, he said, "As I was saying, trials start today. We'll do three at a time twice daily to get through everyone, hopefully in a week or so." Then pointing to Marcus, he said, "You! Find me three prisoners in the pit. Let's get going, shall we?"

"Yes, sir," said Marcus.

Longinus looked at Marcus and nodded in a way that communicated exactly who to choose for trials. At least one of them."

"One more thing," Pilate said. "I'm curious. See what the prisoners know about this Jesus and whether or not he was involved in the rebellion the other night."

The Lucky Three

Marcus and another decurion went down to the pit. Marcus had already known to cover his nose, but it was the first time for the other officer and he began gagging immediately from the stench, not to mention the sight of rats consuming one of the inmates and beginning to nibble on others.

"You never get used to it," Marcus told him. He glanced over at Felix, who was asleep and not looking good at all. Then, addressing all of the pit's occupants, he announced, "Big day today, everyone! We start trials. Any volunteers?"

Some of the prisoners groaned. A few of them shouted, "Pick me! Pick me!" The pit was miserable enough to prefer death. But the method of death silenced the ones who knew better. Still, some hoped to be freed once Pilate heard their case.

"Relax!" Marcus shouted. "I'm kidding about the volunteers. I'm of course going to choose the two men I personally arrested." He motioned for the prison guards to release Barabbas and Ehud from their wall shackles and bind them together.

"Let's have some fun," said Marcus. Addressing Ehud, he said, "Why don't *you* pick the third prisoner for trial today."

Ehud spat on the ground and kicked away a rat. With a slight grin, he said, "Gladly." Then he nodded in Micah's direction.

"I thought you might pick him," said Marcus. "Isn't that your buddy and partner in crime? Nice friend, you are." He instructed the prison guards to release Micah from his wall chains and bind him to the other two.

"Last order of business," Marcus said. "What role did Jesus the

Nazarene play in your failed rebellion? Are any of you aware of this man?"

For a moment, the pit was quiet on the matter. Then a prisoner called out, "He healed my brother of leprosy. Leave that man alone."

"Jesus is a prophet," Barabbas added. "That's what people are saying. Many have reported miracles of various kinds. I wish I could say he was with us. But he had nothing to do with any of this. That, I can assure you."

Marcus nodded and looked around at the desperate faces to see if anyone else had more information.

Another prisoner spoke up and said, "If I tell you what I know, will you release me?"

"That depends on what you know," Marcus said. "Try it and find out."

"I need you to promise you'll release me."

"We promise to *maybe* not kill you right here, right now," said the officer with Marcus. This made the prison guards laugh.

"I'll promise to tell the governor if your information is of any value," Marcus said. "I'll put in a good word. How's that?"

"Alright," the prisoner said. "Here's what I know. With my own ears, I've heard Jesus the Nazarene speak of a new kingdom he wants to establish."

There was silence after this was said. They all looked at one another.

"And?" asked Marcus.

"And what?" the prisoner said. "That's it. That's all I know."

Marcus rolled his eyes and said, "Let's go."

The guards let the decurions and their prisoners out of the pit. Behind them, they heard the inmate shouting, "Tell the governor! You promised! Get me out of here! You have to tell Pilate I helped you!"

The Trial of Thieves

Pilate was laughing and joking with officials. Longinus saw the idle time as an opportunity to address his concerns.

"Governor, may I have a word?" he said quietly.

"Yes, of course. Remind me of your name again."

"Longinus."

"No wonder I forgot it already. Speak your piece."

"It's about this Jesus fellow," Longinus began. "He's a bit different, sir. But he's no criminal. He's actually a good man. He even stopped a woman from being stoned to death."

"That's exactly what I told them," Pilate said. "Were you not listening? I told them he's no criminal and to get out of my face. I sent them off to Herod. You were there. It's his problem, not mine. You say he saved a woman's life?"

"That's right, sir."

"Well, what did she do?" Pilate asked. "Did she deserve to be saved?"

"She was no criminal," Longinus said. "Simply caught up in an angry religious mob, similar to the one today."

"They're the worst kind, are they not?"

"I suppose," said Longinus, growing impatient with Pontius Pilate.

"Well, get on with it," Pilate demanded. "What about this Jesus fellow?"

"Sir, I'm afraid the mob looks particularly determined of his demise, for whatever reason."

"Jupiter only knows. Though I imagine it has something to do with the man threatening their influence and power. They're a jealous bunch."

"If they come back—"

"Come back?" Pilate interrupted. "Why would they come back? Herod will take care of it. He has to. The man is a Galilean. I will lose more hair than I already have if they come back."

Just then, Marcus and the other officer brought in the three prisoners for trial. Pilate saw them and adjusted himself in his chair to sit up straight. He stared them down.

"Well, who's first?" he asked.

Once again, there were no volunteers.

"Is there any present with testimony against one or all of these men?"

Longinus did not want to miss his opportunity for revenge and looked over to Marcus to give testimony.

"Governor, *this* man should be tried first," Marcus started. "His name is Jesus Barabbas. He was caught dressed as a centurion during the rebellion."

"Another Jesus," Pilate said. "You don't say? Are you a king as well?" Barabbas shook his head but did not dare utter a word.

"Did you lead the rebellion?"

"Oh, yes," Ehud interrupted. "He led us straight to our glorious victory. If you can please give him your chair, Governor."

Pontius Pilate was shocked and said nothing for a moment. The tension in the room grew palpable with each passing second. Pilate looked at Ehud and tilted his head. Then suddenly he burst into laughter. Everyone else in the room followed suit.

"That was quite funny," he said. "I should make you my personal entertainer." He pointed to Marcus and said, "Please punch this prisoner in the stomach."

"Yes, sir," said Marcus.

"Not again," said Ehud, as he tried to prepare for the blow.

Marcus did as he was told and this time made sure to hit Ehud a bit harder, causing him to collapse and make Micah and Barabbas fall with him, as they were all still chained together.

"You will speak when I tell you to speak," said Pilate to Ehud. "Is that understood?" But Ehud could not speak at all at this point. "You think you have nothing to lose and that your circumstances are bad now? They can always get worse, my friend. Believe me." He started laughing again and said, "*Perhaps you should give him your chair now*. That was too funny. It truly was. I needed that. You know, in another set of circumstances, I could've made you a lot of money. I mean *a lot* of money. Let's move on, shall we? Where were we?"

"Barabbas," Longinus reminded him.

"Yes, Barabbas."

"I witnessed him commit murder," said Marcus.

"He killed a whore," another officer blurted out. Longinus took note of this man's face, hoping there'd be a time to smash it later that day. "I saw it with my own eyes."

"A whore?" Pilate said. "Did killing this whore shake the Roman Empire? She must've been some whore!"

Barabbas kept quiet and did not look at the governor. His shame returned. He would not be allowed to forget about the innocent woman's life he took. Longinus stared at Barabbas intently, wishing he was the one who could legally sentence him to death. He regretted not killing him in the pit.

"The woman was a Jew," Marcus added.

"Really?" said Pilate. "One of his own. He seems to be confused about who his enemy is."

"He killed some of our soldiers as well," Marcus went on. "And since he was already disguised as a general, he escaped with one of our horses rather easily through the Essene Gate, barking orders at our men in Greek."

"Pretending to be a centurion, then barking orders in Greek," said Pilate. "Rookie mistake. But they let you pass nonetheless?" He called over an officer and whispered in his ear, "When this is over, find the soldiers who fell for this man's dumb trick. Please have them whipped at once." The officer nodded. Pilate continued, "And where was he caught?"

"I found him fighting with *this* prisoner on the other side of the wall near the drainage tunnel," Marcus answered, pointing to Ehud. "They were covered in filth and I arrested both of them on the spot. I presume they are friends."

"We're not friends," said Ehud, still struggling to catch his breath.

"Careful," Pilate said. "You don't want to get punched in the gut again, do you?"

Ehud shook his head.

"A kingdom divided against itself cannot stand. This is common knowledge. And what is *this* man's story?"

Marcus went on to explain how Ehud was caught with several pouches of gold he and Micah had robbed from the house of Caleb the spice merchant. Pilate was well aware of every wealthy family in the city. Marcus described how Micah had even crawled back through the tunnel to retrieve gold he left behind on the other side and that is how he got caught.

"Now that is determination," said Pilate. "But greed gets us every single time. The things we do for money."

"Simon—Caleb's brother—reported the incident," said Marcus. Pointing to Micah, he said, "And we were told *this one* even held a dagger to his young daughter's throat."

Upon hearing this, Pilate motioned to Marcus to punch Micah in the stomach.

Ehud began laughing when all the air left Micah's lungs. He was just catching his breath himself. For good measure, Pilate had Marcus punch Ehud again.

"A little girl?" said Pilate. "Have some standards. Honestly, you are almost as good as what you had to crawl through in the drainage tunnel…Almost. Carry on."

"Other witnesses have come forward and reported these men killed two Upper City watchmen to escape the area. These were men they worked with, as they were Upper City watchmen, themselves. One of my soldiers reported they saw them with Silvanus when the uprising began."

"Stop," Pilate said. "I've heard enough. All three are guilty of insurrection and murder. These two have added robbery to their offenses. And threatening the life of a little girl? Shameful! Prepare them for crucifixion. All execution orders will be signed outside at the Stone Pavement. Get me another three prisoners. I'd like to get done by—"

Pontius Pilate stopped mid-sentence. He arose from his chair and stared past the open entrance of the palace into the distance.

"Do you hear that?" he asked.

All the generals, officials, and soldiers followed Pilate to the entrance of the palace to listen.

Then a huge noisy crowd appeared from around a corner and was coming straight toward them. The multitude with Caiaphas and the Council of Thirteen had now swelled considerably. In front of the angry mob were the same two temple guards holding Jesus the Nazarene at each side.

The King Returns

Jesus was bound and clothed in a royal purple robe. Pontius Pilate laughed immediately. He called over his advisor and said, "Please give word to Herod I'd like to have a meal with him some evening before I leave. This is simply hilarious." Then turning to the rest of his officials, he shouted, "Does Herod not have a great sense of humor?"

The Roman generals and officials began laughing as well. All but Longinus, who understood what this meant even before it was explained. Pilate would have to make the decision. Before the mob reached the Stone Pavement Longinus approached Pilate once again.

"Sir, can I have a word?" he said.

"What do you want now?" Pilate asked.

"This is what I was afraid would happen. They are back because they are determined to have this man executed."

"They are back because Herod saw no evidence worthy of punishment. Nor do I. As far as I can tell, the only thing this man is guilty of is annoying the very people I despise. He deserves a place of honor in my cabinet of advisors. Perhaps I can make him Chief Annoyance Officer. Why do you care so much about this man? Do you know him personally?"

"I've only met him once, sir. It was enough to recognize what kind of man he is."

"Is that so?" Pilate asked. "Just one time, one conversation, and you can tell he does not deserve death. Can you see inside the mind of man? Can you stare into the hidden motives of the heart?"

"No, sir."

"Nor can I. But I do know that we all wear various masks and play different parts in this tragedy called life. Enough talk, they're here. Let's see what happens."

Pilate laughed again when he was able to get a better look at how Herod dressed Jesus.

"You're back," he said. "And I can see Herod honored this man. Maybe you should bow before your king."

The chief priest snarled at the governor. Ithamar then spoke.

"Herod is not in a position to sentence anyone to death. This man has claimed to be the Son of God. According to a law we have, he needs to be executed." Several accusations were made after that. They went on to talk about Jesus inciting riots.

"Do you not hear what these men are saying?" Pilate asked Jesus. "They want you dead. What do you have to say for yourself?"

Jesus did not respond. Pilate was astonished at his silence. When he saw the crowd had grown larger and even more restless and rowdy, he walked back inside the palace to his chair. He summoned Jesus in for private questioning.

Jesus was still bound and held by the two temple guards. The one with the bloody ear served Caiaphas directly and was named Malchus. When Longinus took the arm of Jesus, Malchus dropped to his knees and began to weep.

"What is the meaning of this?" Caiaphas asked. But Malchus wept all the more.

Jesus said to Malchus, "Arise, my son, your sins are forgiven." This caused an immediate uproar.

"Do we need any more evidence against this man?" they began to shout. Several men tried hitting Jesus and almost caused the two large centurions to stumble.

"Enough!" Longinus shouted as he shoved men to the ground with ease. Malchus took off running. "If you don't all calm down, I'll personally throw you in the pit. Is that understood?"

Caiaphas got his men to relax and give room for the centurions to do their job.

As they made their way to Pontius Pilate, Longinus ever so discreetly whispered in the ear of Jesus, "Keep calm. I've been trying to get you out of this. Pilate has no intention to execute you."

The centurions led Jesus directly in front of Pontius Pilate. The governor looked Jesus up and down. Everyone in the room fixed their eyes on Jesus, including the three prisoners already sentenced to death.

"So," Pilate began. "Are you an idiot or something? You hear these men making all sorts of accusations. Are you mute? Have you no ability to defend yourself? I'm giving you the chance to do that."

Jesus said nothing at first. Pilate looked at his men and said, "Unbelievable." Then turning back to Jesus, he said, "Are you or are you not the king of the Jews?"

Jesus finally spoke and told Pilate how his kingdom was not of this world.

"Aha!" Pilate said. "So you do claim to be a king."

But Jesus of Nazareth simply repeated how his kingdom was not from this world.

Pilate looked at him curiously and said, "This is the only world I know, my friend. If you come from another one, then that has nothing to do with me, does it?"

Jesus and Pilate then discussed the issue of truth and how Pilate would understand if he were on the side of truth.

"Truth?" Pilate said. "What is truth? Do you hear that crowd out there?" He stood up and pointed to the open palace entrance. "A rebellion is about to start. That is the truth I'm concerned about, my friend."

Pilate looked over at Longinus and remembered his conversation. He sat back down.

"I have an idea," said Pilate. "Which of these three prisoners is the worst?" He pointed to Barabbas, Ehud, and Micah, still chained to one another and guarded by soldiers, listening to this entire conversation. "Surely it's the one who put a dagger to a little girl's throat."

Micah dropped his head in shame.

"No," said Marcus. "It is Jesus Barabbas." He looked at Longinus and winked. "It was Barabbas who led the rebellion, incited people to riot, murdered innocent women, and even killed some of our men. I would not be surprised if he ordered the robbery of Caleb. Remember, these three men are friends, sir."

"Yes, that is true," said Pilate. "That does make sense. Very well, unchain Barabbas from the other prisoners. We will go back outside. I want you to position one Jesus on my right side and the other to my left. We will settle this once and for all. Let the people decide. This man's accusers will have to deal with the outcome."

Longinus made sure he was the one to lead Barabbas.

"Seeing you up there on that cross will be the highlight of my day," he said. "I'll get the honey ready."

"For his bits," Marcus added with a chuckle. "A feast for the birds of prey. Or perhaps a light snack."

Two Jesuses

There was a moment inside the palace when Pilate and his men got ready to face the crowd. Pilate spoke with his council of advisors about exactly how he should present the case and ensure everyone was satisfied with the outcome and no uprising began.

During this time, Jesus Barabbas and Jesus the Nazarene were chained to one another, a centurion on each side.

Doing his best to ignore Longinus, who was holding his arm tight enough to stop blood flow, Barabbas turned his head to look at the famous Jesus of Nazareth he'd heard so much about over the past year.

Neither of these men looked impressive. Barabbas was a bit chubbier and taller, but not by much. He was also considerably filthier than Jesus from his time in the pit. Both had facial injuries from beatings, though the wounds on the Nazarene were only hours old.

"Rabbi, I've been wanting to meet you for a very long time," Barabbas said. "I was hoping you would join us. But better late than never." Then ever so quietly, Barabbas tried to whisper in the direction of Jesus low enough so the centurions couldn't hear. This was no easy task. He said, "When are they coming?"

Jesus turned toward Barabbas and whispered back, "Who?"

"Your followers. When are they coming? Isn't that why you've come? To overthrow—?" Barabbas did not want to say it. He simply pointed with his eyes at the Romans surrounding them.

"I've come to overthrow the wickedness in your heart," said Jesus.

Barabbas looked down, frustrated.

"You are only a teacher," he said, no longer whispering. "Nothing anyone should feel threatened by. They're making a big mistake out there. You don't belong here with me. I have no doubt I'll get what I deserve. I knew this day was coming. For years I knew this day was coming. I told myself it would be worth it in the end. No matter the cost, no matter the sacrifice. Our land has been defiled for too long. Ridding it of Roman oppressors and establishing a new kingdom was worth my life. That's what I told myself. But now I'm not sure. My wife will be a widow. My children will be fatherless. I only hope they'll one day see what I did for our people. What I did for them...What I at least *tried* to do for them. Though I accomplished nothing it seems."

Jesus the Nazarene turned to Barabbas and asked, "Can a kingdom of peace be established through violence?"

Barabbas was a bit taken aback by the question and said, "Rabbi, is there any other way to establish a new kingdom? All kingdoms must be established by force. I heard you tell Pilate *your* kingdom is from another place. What did you mean by that if you haven't come to overthrow anything? Where is this place? Surely the Romans are not there."

"I told the truth when I said my kingdom is not of this world," Jesus said. "The world works by the powerful subjecting the weak. That is the law in every land. Greed, selfish ambition, lust, and bloodshed. You are right when you say the kingdoms of *this* world are established by force."

"And how does the kingdom in *your* world work?" Barabbas asked. "What is the law of that land?"

"Love."

Barabbas stared at Jesus for a moment.

"I heard you speak in riddles," he said. "But I think I understand. You are not speaking of a *real* kingdom, are you?"

"Love is more real than the chains that bind us?" said Jesus.

Barabbas thought about that. He wriggled his wrists around in the shackles. He felt the tightness of the centurion's grip on his arm. Nothing felt more real than his current predicament and imminent death. Still, he wondered what it would be like to believe in something different. He was finally in a situation where there was truly nothing to lose for doing so. He could see no risk at this point. The worst had already happened, or at least was slated to happen later that day.

"If what you say is true," replied Barabbas, "if love is more real than these chains, then I wish for love to free me from these chains. If love is what your kingdom is about, and you are the ruler of this kingdom, then please, let me have another chance at life. Surely, if you are a king of love," Barabbas hesitated before finishing his sentence, "then you must be full of mercy. I ask that you free me from these chains, though I don't deserve it. I've heard amazing things about you. Stories of healing, raising the dead, and feeding thousands with hardly any food. Surely God is with you and has given you the power to release me. I imagine you even have the power to release yourself. Again, I don't deserve freedom. I know that. I killed an innocent woman. One of our own. I didn't mean to." Barabbas wept but went on. "That doesn't matter, does it? She's gone and I killed her. I've killed others as well. But I believe you can unshackle these chains. If you can do that, then I believe you can change my heart and life as well…if you are willing, of course."

Jesus smiled and said, "According to your faith, so be it unto you, Barabbas. Go and sin no more."

Barabbas wanted it to be true with everything in him. He moved his wrists around. They were still bound. Not only that, but Longinus had been listening to their conversation and was not happy about it one bit.

He leaned over to whisper to Barabbas, "The only thing that will be freed today is your soul from your body. I will personally make sure of that." Barabbas said nothing. But he no longer felt defeated. Something was stirring inside of him.

"Time to face the lunacy!" Pilate announced.

The Romans led the two prisoners out to the Stone Pavement. Pilate sat in the judgment seat. Jesus Barabbas was placed on his left side, Jesus of Nazareth on his right.

"What is the meaning of this?" the chief priest asked.

"As tradition holds," Pilate began, "I have been in the gracious custom of releasing one prisoner during your annual Passover festival. This year will be no different. I present to you—not one—but two Jesuses." Pilate then waited for the booing to stop. "Now before you choose, let us examine the crimes of each. Here on my right is Jesus the Nazarene. He has been accused of rebellion. However, prisoners in the pit were interviewed and not one had any knowledge of his involvement in the failed insurrection the other day. The kingdom he speaks of is merely a parable. He poses no threat to Rome and no threat to you. To my left is Jesus Barabbas. Now this man was caught in the very act of rebelling against Roman authority, inciting a riot, and murdering—not only some of my men—but also one of your own. A defenseless woman nonetheless. He is a despicable failure of a man. He is a friend to neither Roman nor Jew."

Barabbas kept his head down and could not face the crowd.

"So I ask," Pilate said to the multitude, "now that you have all the information you need, who would you like freed this day in keeping with my Passover tradition of mercy: Jesus of Nazareth, in whom neither myself nor Herod could find fault with, or Jesus Barabbas, a rebel, a rioter, an insurrectionist, a friend of thieves, and a murderer of his own people?"

"Barabbas," the chief priest said. Then he looked at the crowd and shouted, "Free Barabbas!" Soon, the entire crowd was shouting, "Free Barabbas! Free Barabbas!"

Longinus felt a mix of fear and fury welling up within him. Barabbas lifted his head in disbelief, then looked toward Jesus who showed no emotion whatsoever. Pilate looked on in utter shock. Just then, Pilate's personal servant came up to him with a message from his wife that read, "Have nothing to do with this innocent man. I had nightmares all last night about him."

Pilate said to the servant, "Please tell my wife to mind her own business. I have enough trouble today. I don't need her superstitions added to it."

"Yes, sir."

"Everybody back inside!" shouted Pilate over the roar of the crowd.

The prisoners were taken back into the palace. However, Pilate and a couple of his guards and advisors stayed behind.

"I wish to speak with Caiaphas alone," Pilate told one of his officers.

They summoned Caiaphas to come forward. Pilate stood up from the judgment seat.

"I cannot enter the palace," Caiaphas said.

"I know, I know," said Pilate. "Ceremonial uncleanness. Your followers may think of you as less than priestly. We wouldn't want that. Let's talk and walk for a moment, shall we?"

The two men began walking in front of the palace with Roman guards and advisors following closely behind.

"What is the meaning of this?" asked Pilate.

"The meaning of what?" asked Caiaphas. "You brought out two prisoners. You told us to choose which one we wanted released. We followed your orders and chose."

"You chose a man guilty of great crimes. I only brought him out so you can see the absurdity of it all. Why do you want the Nazarene dead so bad? What has he done to you?"

"We've already told you, Governor. He has claimed to be the Son of God, a crime we deem worthy of death. Now perhaps you think of that as a trivial matter having no significance, but may I remind you, he calls himself a king."

"Yes," Pilate said, "But not a *real* king. More like a pretend make-believe king. He's absolutely crazy but not dangerous."

"His followers are not pretending, I assure you. They intend to overthrow you. His numbers grow each day."

"Oh, and I'm sure you would never want to see me nor any Roman authority overthrown, now would you?" The chief priest did not respond. "You want to know what I think, Caiaphas? I think you're jealous of the man. He's not a rule-follower. He doesn't play your game. The people like him more than they like you. Am I right?"

Caiaphas glared at Pontius Pilate, and then to the crowd, still shouting, "Free Barabbas!"

"Governor, these people look very restless. What would Tiberius think if another riot took place? What would happen to you if he found out you were unfit to rule?"

"Are you threatening me?" Pilate asked.

"Never!" said Caiaphas. "Far be it from me to threaten any Roman authority! I'm simply wondering aloud. How could any Roman leader release a man claiming to be king and who teaches the people to stop paying taxes to Caesar? Does not such a man oppose Caesar? Wouldn't failing to respond mean that you also oppose Caesar? I imagine you're the kind of man who deals with such problems as swiftly as possible—someone who showcases his power and authority and makes examples of treasonous criminals. You're not a leader who lets troublemakers get away with anything. That's for sure."

Pilate did not respond to this.

"I should get going," Caiaphas said. "The crowd grows restless by the minute. I'll see what I can do to calm them. I trust you'll make the right decision, Governor."

The chief priest returned to the Council of Thirteen standing before the raucous crowd. Pontius Pilate looked over to one of his advisors.

"They will stir up trouble for you," the advisor said.

"Really?" Pilate said with obvious sarcasm. "Is that what I pay you for? To tell me the things that are as clear as day? Let's go inside. I need a drink."

Justice

Barabbas stared at Jesus with his mouth open. He couldn't seem to close it. They were still chained together, waiting for Pilate to finish deliberating with his council of advisors. Longinus squeezed his arm even tighter,

"If by some miracle," Longinus said, "this all works out for you, I will hunt you down personally and give you the execution you justly deserve. So either way, your fate is sealed. You will not see the light of tomorrow."

Longinus tried to stare into the eyes of Barabbas, but he noticed the eyes of Jesus were staring at *him*. He looked at the Nazarene and a wave of shame and guilt washed over him. Longinus had to look away for a moment. He wasn't quite sure why, but he could not look upon the face of Jesus. He suddenly realized how powerless he was to rescue Jesus from his unwarranted dilemma. He looked over at Pontius Pilate talking with his advisors and wondered why the governor could not realize the same thing.

"Barabbas, I swear," said Ehud, who was off to the side and still chained to Micah, "if you are not executed with us, I will come back as a ghost from Sheol to haunt you and your family for the rest of your life."

"That seems to be a common sentiment today," said Barabbas.

After a few more moments passed, Pilate announced, "Let us try reason once more, shall we?"

Pontius Pilate, along with some of his soldiers, generals, officers, and advisors went back outside the palace to present Jesus and Barabbas again. The crowd was somehow even more restless than before. Caiaphas and the others stared calmly at the governor.

Pilate raised his hand to silence the crowd, which only worked when the high priest did the same. This annoyed the governor. With a loud voice, he said, "In keeping with my annual tradition of mercy and pardon toward you fine people of Jerusalem, I present to you—once again—a choice between two prisoners to be set free this day. Jesus Barabbas is an enemy of both Romans and Jews. Jesus the Nazarene—on the other hand—poses no real threat to either."

Before Pilate could finish articulating his appeal, the crowd was stirred to shout, "Free Barabbas! Free Barabbas!"

"But why?" Pilate shouted back. "*He* is the criminal. Not the Nazarene." But the crowd had no interest in hearing anything he had to say.

The Romans stared at them blankly in bewilderment.

"Well," Caiaphas said, "We've made our choice. By your own law, you must honor it."

Pilate looked to his council of advisors for help. The lead advisor nodded to him as a signal for the governor's next move.

Pontius Pilate asked for a bowl of water to be brought to him. A servant promptly obeyed. Pilate dipped his hands in the water and rubbed them together, pretending to wash off his guilt in front of the crowd.

"I am innocent of this man's blood," he said. "It is your responsibility." He shook the water off into the chief priest's face. Longinus looked down, knowing exactly how the rest of the day would unfold.

Pilate walked over to Barabbas and quietly said, "If you ever again get into the slightest of trouble, if I hear the whisper of your name in accusation, whether true or false, you will not be presented to anyone but my torturers and executioners. Is that understood?"

Barabbas nodded but didn't speak.

Pilate walked back to his judgment seat and sat down.

"Release Jesus Barabbas!" he announced. The crowd roared.

It was all Longinus could do to keep himself from screaming out of sheer frustration.

The guard with the key to the shackles came forward and gave it to Longinus. Longinus was shaking as he inserted the key into the keyhole. He looked up at Barabbas and whispered, "This is not over."

Barabbas was released from his shackles but felt released from so much more. Longinus gave him a shove to the ground. Instead of getting up immediately, Barabbas turned to Jesus and bowed his head toward the Nazarene's feet. Then he looked up and said, "Thank you." Jesus smiled. A few members of the Council of Thirteen and a temple guard pulled Barabbas to his feet and threw him into the crowd, saying, "Now go away before we charge you with blasphemy!"

Pointing to Jesus, Pilate asked, "And now what shall I do with this one?" The chief priest and his secret council stirred the entire crowd to shout back, "Crucify him!"

Pilate waved his hand to dismiss them and announced, "I will have him flogged. He'll receive thirty-nine lashes according to your own law, but no more!" Then turning to Longinus, he said, "Please oversee the flogging. Let me know when it's done." Pilate stood up from the judgment seat. The people were still shouting and chanting, "Crucify him!"

"But, sir," Longinus began.

Pilate gave him a stern look and Longinus did not finish his sentence. The governor and his council of advisors went back inside the palace before everyone else. Longinus looked at the crowd to see where Barabbas ran off to. But he was now lost in the sea of people. He then grabbed a soldier and ordered him to locate Barabbas and report to him later with his whereabouts.

"Meet me by the stables when my shift is finished," Longinus commanded. "Tell no one what I asked of you." The soldier promptly left to search for Barabbas.

Longinus then took the arm of Jesus with hardly any pressure at all and led him into the palace to be flogged.

His head was spinning when he walked into the main hall. His ruined eye began to throb with ferocious pain that radiated across the side of his face and head. He dropped to one knee when he lost his balance. Concerned, Marcus ran up to Longinus and asked if he was alright.

"I'm not feeling well, Marcus. Can you oversee the flogging? Let me catch my breath for a moment."

"Of course," said Marcus. "Shall I send for the doctor? Though, I never know where he is."

"No," Longinus answered. "Just go. I'll be fine."

Marcus helped his mentor to his feet, then led Jesus to the floggers. Longinus followed close behind but hid in the shadows outside the roofless punishment room. He heard the mockery of the soldiers as they pretended to treat Jesus as a king.

"Hail, your majesty!" was said several times. There was punching and slapping, but Jesus did not make a sound. Only when the flogging began did Jesus scream. Longinus covered his ears. This muffled the noise but didn't mute it. Squeezing his good eye shut caused his bad eye to rage with pain. Longinus knew the soldiers were using the flagrums he instructed them to when he showed Marcus around the palace. He wanted to stop the injustice of it all but felt powerless. Instead, he slid his back down the stone wall and sat on the cold floor, alone in the shadows. He began to count lashes and prayed for thirty-nine to come quicker than usual.

Why is this taking so long? he thought.

But lash thirty-nine finally did come and along with it a hush.

Longinus felt empty. He did his best to compose himself and slowly stood to his feet. He did not feel like a centurion anymore. Something inside of him was lost forever.

Longinus stepped out of the shadows and into the punishment room. There Jesus was, face down in the middle of the courtyard. His back and sides were torn to shreds. Upon his head was a crown of thorns the soldiers had fashioned as a joke. It was hard not to step on the blood, though much of it had already been absorbed by the earth.

The mockery had stopped and the soldiers quieted themselves at the sight of their superior. Marcus came over to Longinus to casually ask how he was feeling, unmoved by everything that had just taken place.

Longinus did not answer. He swallowed hard and quietly commanded two soldiers, "Help the man to his feet."

Jesus was unconscious and his body was limp. Longinus did his best to wake him but had to wait a few moments before returning him to the governor.

Power

Pontius Pilate was once again joking with his council of advisors when Jesus the Nazarene was brought back to him. He was shocked at the sight. He normally did not have to see anyone after they were flogged. Pilate simply gave his orders and thought no more of the individual. The words of his wife's message were ringing in his head. He even thought about his conversation with Longinus. But it was Caiaphas who he most wanted to demonstrate his power to. Pilate stood from his chair. His council of advisors grimaced and turned away when they saw Jesus.

Longinus took a step back from the prisoner to allow the governor to examine him. Jesus collapsed to his knees when he did so.

"The order was to flog him, not turn him into raw meat," said Pilate. "He can't even stand."

"He received a standard flogging, sir," said Longinus.

Pilate grunted. He walked around Jesus to look at his backside where most of his injuries were. He regretted it instantly. "This is more for people who would put a dagger to a little girl's throat." Pilate glanced coldly at Micah when he said this. Ehud was smart enough to keep his mouth shut this time. "Help him to his feet," Pilate said to Longinus. "Someone put Herod's robe back on him. Caiaphas is not going to tell me what to do with prisoners. I will not be manipulated! Let us see if they still think he is such a threat now."

The governor and his entourage walked out to the Stone Pavement. Pilate motioned to Jesus and proclaimed in a loud voice,

"Here is the man! As a token of good faith toward you fine people, I've punished him." Pilate then instructed Longinus to remove the purple robe from Jesus and show the crowd his shredded back. Longinus held Jesus steady the whole time.

The people let out a gasp of disgust. Even Caiaphas and the others were taken aback for a moment. But they collected themselves quickly and said, "Crucify him!"

Pilate very much wished he could punish the entire Sanhedrin and everyone with the high priest to demonstrate his power over them once and for all. Instead, he pleaded with them, saying, "But why? What has this man done worthy of death? Look at him! He has been punished enough already. Herod saw no fault in him. Neither do I. You take him and crucify him. My part is finished. I've already washed my hands from this man's blood. I have nothing to do with this."

That last statement disgusted Longinus. The centurion saw Pilate as no better than a puppet on a string to be moved this way and that. Annas, the chief priest's father-in-law, reminded Pilate that Jesus claimed to be the Son of God and therefore must die according to their law.

Pilate walked over to Longinus and said, "Bring the Nazarene back into the palace. I wish to speak with him privately. The voice of the shouting crowd felt like a unified force, shaking the very foundation of the palace.

The governor stood in front of Jesus once again and looked at him.

"So what is it about you?" he asked. "What do you expect me to do? You're not helping me get you out of this. If I do nothing, Caiaphas will lead a revolt right here, right now. He'll have his fabricated crowd of madmen storm the palace. Then what?"

Jesus said nothing.

"Now is *not* the time for silence!" Pilate shouted. "Or do you not realize that I and I alone have the power to free or crucify you?"

Shaking through the pain and loss of blood, Jesus informed Pilate that the only power he had was that which God granted to him. Pilate looked at Jesus with astonishment. The last thing he wanted to hear at that moment was that he had no power.

"Stay here for a moment," he told Jesus and Longinus. He walked back outside to meet with the accusers.

"I've examined the man thoroughly. I've questioned him.

Insurrectionists in the pit have been questioned as well. I find no basis for a charge against him. I'm releasing the half-dead Nazarene."

"Release him," Caiaphas said, "and you will be an enemy of Caesar just like him because he claims to be a king." Caiaphas and his followers then had the crowd begin shouting chants about Pilate being an enemy of Caesar and Rome.

Pilate walked up to whisper in the ear of Caiaphas, "This is not a real crowd. You know it. I know it. Only a few short days ago, the people were welcoming this man into the city like he was royalty. Now you expect me to believe they all hate him. No. This mob is bought and paid for."

Caiaphas stared into the governor's eyes and said, "If what you say is true—if you're suggesting I paid for this crowd—wouldn't that mean they are still mine to do my bidding? Wouldn't that mean that whatever we tell them to do, they will do? If I tell them to shout something, they'll shout it. If I tell them to storm the palace, they'll do it."

"Is that a confession?" Pilate asked.

"Believe what you wish to believe. Do what you wish to do. You're the governor. You have the power. I'm sure Tiberius will hear of your strong and wise leadership either way."

Longinus was not sure if he should speak to Jesus or not. The other two prisoners were being closely guarded not far off. But in the main hall of the palace, it was just the two of them, waiting for Pilate to return for further instructions. He decided to finally look at the Nazarene's face. The crown of thorns had caused several beads of blood to run down his head on all sides. There were bumps and bruises and more injuries than Longinus could count.

"I tried to speak to the governor for you," he began, rather awkwardly. "You don't deserve this. I know that much. I don't know what I was expecting Pilate to do. Certainly not this. I'm just following orders. I don't have a choice. I hope you understand."

Jesus looked at the large centurion in his one good eye and said, "Love your enemies and do good to those who hate you and to those whom you hate."

"Why would anyone do that?" Longinus asked.

"Vengeance is poison," Jesus answered. "The pain you inflict on others will always return to you. Therefore love your neighbor as yourself."

Longinus looked away. He was stunned. He waited a moment before speaking again.

"You truly are crazy," he finally said. A soldier then came into the palace to summon them.

When they walked out, the crowd was even rowdier than before. Pontius Pilate was sitting in the judge's seat at the Stone Pavement. When he saw Jesus come out, he shouted, "Behold, your king!"

"Take him away!" the people shouted. "Crucify him!"

"Is that how you treat your king? Shall I crucify your king?" Agitating the accusers was all Pilate wanted to do for the rest of the day. He saw no better way to accomplish this than to constantly refer to Jesus as *The King of the Jews*.

"We have no king but Caesar!" they shouted back.

Pilate raised his hand to silence the crowd. Once again, Caiaphas had to assist the governor in this.

"You have made your choice of pardon today," Pilate began. "I have washed my hands of guilt in your presence and have transferred the responsibility to you fine people." He paused and took a deep breath. "The Nazarene will be executed!" The crowd shouted in triumph and raised their fists in the air. Caiaphas looked at the governor and nodded in approval. Pilate turned to Longinus and the other generals and officers present and said, "Well, go on. Get him out of here. Crucify him with the other two." Then he called for a servant to make sure a notice was attached to the top of the cross that read, *This is the King of the Jews*.

"Make sure it's big and clear," Pilate said. "I want Caiaphas and the rest of them to see it. Also, have someone fetch me a bowl of grapes and some wine."

Second Chance

Barabbas was already outside of the city gates. He heard when the people shouted, "We have no king but Caesar." Under his breath, he said, "We have no king but God." Then he left Jerusalem almost skipping back to his house. At one point, he couldn't contain his joy and began to run.

When Barabbas's wife Deborah learned of her husband's arrest, she began to prepare herself to live life as a widow. She always knew that was more than possible. All of the wives of Zealots did. She and her husband spoke of it often. But now Deborah had no idea how she would survive. She only hoped her husband's wealthy contacts would take care of her and the children out of respect. Barabbas assured her they would, but Deborah was not convinced.

So seeing Barabbas walk through the threshold was a bit like seeing a ghost. Deborah could not believe her eyes.

"Barabbas?" she said. She leaned forward and squinted to make sure. "It is you!" She ran up and they embraced. Barabbas laughed and lifted his wife in the air. He swung her around in a circle. Their three small children ran up to wrap their arms around his legs, shouting, "Abba!"

"What happened?" Deborah asked. "Did you escape? Do we have to run away right now? Children, we're leaving! Let's go!"

"No, no, no," Barabbas said with a chuckle. "Relax. We're not running away. Pilate released me." He went on to explain all the events that took place. The rebellion, the pit, Ehud and Micah, and finally his encounter with Jesus of Nazareth.

"They've arrested the prophet?" Deborah asked.

"He's being executed today," Barabbas said. "It's wrong. He is more than a prophet. He is the one who truly released me. Not Pilate."

He went on to explain how he would no longer be a Zealot but instead live his life for God by being upright and honest. He would strive to be good and generous and at peace with everyone. Never again will he hurt or kill unless in defense of his loved ones.

Barabbas saw a new future for his family. He saw the opportunity of a fresh start. He saw how he would now spend his time training his children to love their neighbor. He saw how he would treat his wife and never intentionally put her at risk of becoming a widow. He saw a new life he couldn't help but whisper a prayer of gratitude for.

What Barabbas did not see was the Roman soldier who had followed him from a distance all the way to his home.

Part Three

Golgotha

Simon and Dinah arose early to hear Jesus speak that morning. They agreed to finally approach the prophet when he had a free moment. They wanted to officially let him know they were now his followers. They couldn't agree as to whom or how they should donate their wealth. Though he had already made his previous announcement, they still had not told Caleb and Leah their intention to actually go through with it, nor did they tell their children. Preparing for the Sabbath did not seem like the right time to make such contentious announcements. Simon thought it best to let his brother know right before sailing home, in case he never wanted to speak with him again. As for now, Caleb and Leah hoped this fanatic phase would pass.

"Where are you two off again?" Leah asked. "Don't tell me, I already know. Your secret is safe with me. But please don't be long, there's much to do."

"We'll be back soon enough," said Simon. Then turning to his wife, he said, "Tell the boys to come with us. I want them to hear as well. But leave Joanna. She should stay and help Leah."

Simon, Dinah, and the twins arrived at the temple but Jesus was not in his usual place where he delivered sermons to both his disciples and strangers. They searched all around the temple and surrounding area but the Nazarene was nowhere to be found. They asked several people but no one seemed to know his whereabouts.

"Perhaps he and his disciples have more important things to

do," suggested Dinah.

"Yes, perhaps," said Simon. "But I was hoping to speak with him today."

"He might be watching the trials," a stranger said, overhearing the conversation. "There's a huge crowd gathered at the palace."

"Abba, can we watch the trials?" the boys pleaded.

Simon shook his head.

"Absolutely not," he told them. "Why do you think we took the long way to the temple? I wanted to avoid all that commotion. The brute will probably execute someone today. If I know Pilate, that's exactly what he'll do. No regard for our holy days or anything sacred. Jesus is staying in Bethany somewhere. Boys, you'll come with me. Your mother will go back."

"Are you sure?" Dinah asked. "Maybe you should not bother him. We can find him another day."

"I have no intention of bothering him," said Simon. "I only wish to let him know our plans and ask how our wealth can be distributed to the poor properly."

The boys looked at one another in disbelief.

"So much for keeping that a secret till we leave," Dinah said. She gave her husband a look of admonishment.

"If my family did not believe my first announcement, that isn't my fault. Furthermore, I'm not ashamed to follow the Lord in whatever way I'm called to," he said. "I will certainly not shy away from training my family to do the same. If my brother has a problem with that, so be it."

Dinah said nothing and instead embraced her husband. She still had reservations about their upcoming decisions. But she was somehow overcome with a sense of adventure rather than loss. She knew the Lord would provide for whatever journey he called them to. She went back to Caleb's home to help Leah.

Bethany was less than two miles from the city. Simon insisted they walk rather than take any of Caleb's horses.

But Jesus was not in Bethany either.

"Maybe he left, Father."

"I don't think so," said Simon. "Why would he leave before Passover?"

"Who are you looking for?" a visibly distraught man asked them.

Startled, Simon said, "Oh, hello there. I'm looking for Jesus of

Nazareth, the prophet."

"He's not here," the man said. "He was arrested in Gethsemane early in the morning, hours before dawn."

"Arrested?" Simon said incredulously. "For what? And how do you know this?"

The man began to weep bitterly, then said, "I was there when it happened. I ran like a coward. All three of us did. Peter was the only one brave enough to draw his sword. I don't know where John is. I'm the worst of them, though."

"I don't know any of these people you speak of. Where is Jesus now?"

"I just came back from the palace. I was hiding behind pillars like a scared little boy. Pilate's going to execute him today."

The words crashed into Simon's mind like a tidal wave. He thought of the trials and the crowd gathered at the palace earlier. It can't be, he thought.

"I must find him," said Simon. "This has to be one huge mistake. I will pay everything I have for his release." Simon never felt more sure about anything. Now he knew exactly where his wealth would go if that's what it took to free the prophet. It all made sense now. Jesus was poor. He was also in a helpless situation. Finally, Simon could offer everything he had to help someone other than himself. And what better person to help than the man who changed his life?

"Boys, we're leaving," he said.

"If you find him," the man said, grabbing Simon's arm, "please tell him James is deeply sorry for abandoning him in his time of need. I will never forgive myself." The man could barely finish his sentence and broke down into bitter tears again. He ran away, covering his eyes with his arm. Simon watched him till he disappeared around a corner.

"Come on," he said to his sons. "We have to hurry."

Simon and the boys ran from Bethany on the less-crowded countryside road as fast as they could. They still managed to clumsily knock over carts and bump into people along the way.

They passed through Gethsemane. Simon was suddenly overcome with inexplicable sorrow and grief and didn't know why. He almost collapsed. His sons grabbed his arms to steady him. Simon had to catch his breath for a moment. The voice of the angry mob was carried on the wind.

"Listen," he said. "Do you hear that, boys?" His sons stopped to listen. "It's the execution crowd. It'll take too long to go through the city. We have to go around the wall. They're already on their way to Golgotha."

They ran around the wall and came to a small hill that resembled somewhat of a skull. This was Golgotha, where crucifixions were held. No one had arrived yet. Simon looked down the road and saw the multitude coming. There were Roman soldiers, religious leaders, and a crowd of curious onlookers. Simon noticed the tops of wooden crosses jutting out above everyone's heads.

"There they are," he said. "They just left the city." He took off running again. His young, agile sons struggled to keep up and loved every minute of the adventure, not completely understanding what had come over their father.

The mass of people was thick and impenetrable. Simon grew indignant. He shoved men, women, and children out of his way and forced himself to where the Romans led their prisoners. The twins looked at one another in astonishment. Simon stood in front of the whole procession.

"Stop!" he shouted at them. Surprisingly, the Romans stopped and put their hands on the hilt of their swords. Simon was unafraid and looked at the three faces of the prisoners carrying wooden crosses on their backs. He recognized Ehud and Micah immediately and nodded in approval. But the man who fell facedown into the dirt road, he did not recognize. His face was too battered and covered in blood to do so. His back looked grotesque. Simon had to avert his eyes.

"What have you done with the prophet?" he asked the first centurion he saw, not realizing it was the very one he bumped into by the temple a few days prior. "I'm looking for Jesus of Nazareth. I've come to pay for his release. I'll pay any price." The centurion removed his helmet. Only then did Simon recognize him. A wave of fear sobered him up instantly. He came to his senses and saw the absurdity of his self-imposed predicament.

Longinus remembered Simon as well. He rarely forgot a face. He gave his helmet to a soldier to hold as it was rubbing against his wound and irritating it.

"Well, you're in luck," said Longinus. "You found him."

Simon looked down at the man on the ground.

"It can't be," he said. "Jesus? Is that truly you?"

Jesus did not answer.

"It's him," said Longinus. "Now pick up his cross and help him carry it."

Simon was shocked at the request.

"You're making a joke," he said. "It's not funny. I've come to buy this man's freedom. I can pay anything."

"I'm sure you can," said Longinus. "Pick up his cross."

"I will do no such thing. Tell me the price of this man's freedom and I will pay it. You can't treat me like a criminal."

"I will treat you a lot worse than that if you don't shut up and pick up that cross right now."

"But you don't understand," Simon continued to protest. "I'm not even from here. I live in Cyrene. I'm only here for Passover. I'm staying with my brother, Caleb. Surely you know him. I can make you a rich man. I have more gold than you could possibly imagine."

Longinus looked at Simon, bewildered at his bold persistence.

"*You're* the one who doesn't seem to understand," Longinus said. "Your money is powerless here. No amount will free him. Now help him carry his cross, or I'll personally nail you to the other side of it."

Simon looked back at his horrified sons.

"We have to go," he told Longinus, having a sudden change of heart. "I apologize. I have much to do."

Simon turned to walk away but Longinus stopped him and threw him to the ground. There was no getting out of it. That much was clear. Slowly, without looking up, Simon rose to his hands and knees. He then wrapped his hands around the wooden cross and placed it on his shoulder.

"This isn't right," he said. "None of this is right." Simon looked back at his boys and said, "Alexander and Rufus, go at once and tell your mother what happened to me. Tell your uncle too." The boys took off running to do just that.

Longinus helped Jesus to his feet.

"You've got some help now," said Longinus. "It's not a far walk."

Jesus was positioned in front so Simon could see when he was about to fall. The march to Golgotha resumed. As they walked, Simon asked, "What have they done to you?"

Jesus did not respond. Simon kept talking.

"None of this is right. They're treating you like a common criminal. Now they're treating me like one as well."

"Simon," Jesus said.

"Rabbi?"

"You wanted to find me, here I am. You wanted to follow me, here you are."

Simon thought about it and said, "I certainly did not have *this* in mind."

Jesus was about to fall from sheer exhaustion again.

"Steady now," said Simon. "I'm here. We can rest for a moment if you need. To hell with these Romans."

Jesus looked back at Simon, who felt his rebuke instantly.

They passed by women wailing and mourning. Jesus told them to stop and that they should rather mourn for the future generations who are yet to be born.

"For if the people do these things when the tree is green," Jesus said, "what will happen when it is dry?"

As they approached Golgotha, Simon wanted to tell Jesus all the things on his heart and how he had finally decided to give the entirety of his wealth to the poor and follow him wherever he went. He was suddenly overwhelmed with grief. It was the same grief that struck him when he and the twins passed through Gethsemane. The thought occurred to Simon that all was lost.

"Rabbi," he said. "I was prepared to follow you for the rest of my life. I was prepared to pay everything I have for your release. What will I do now? Go back to making money? Is there nothing else to life?"

Longinus ordered soldiers to take the cross off of the backs of Jesus and Simon and dig holes in the ground, for they arrived at the skull-shaped hill.

As Jesus stood there waiting for the inevitable, he smiled ever so slightly at Simon and said, "Great is your faith, my son. I will be with you always and you will follow me all the days of your life."

Simon said nothing. He stood there staring at Jesus in disbelief at everything unfolding before his eyes. Longinus noticed him not leaving and said, "Now go on! Get out of here!" He gave Simon a shove. Simon backed up but he did not leave. He wasn't sure if he should stay and watch such a gruesome execution. He had no desire to. But he felt he owed it to Jesus to not leave his side until he breathed his last. Simon then looked at the other two men, also waiting for their ends to come. He and Micah made eye contact. They stared at one another, not sure if anything should be said.

"I suppose this doesn't matter right now," said Micah, "but I apologize. My actions were despicable. Forgive me, if you can."

Simon did not respond to this, but Ehud did.

"Oh, shut up already," he said. "You put a blade to his daughter's throat. Are you suddenly repentant? If we were not arrested and sentenced to death, we'd probably be robbing someone else right now. Go ahead, start talking about your mommy. What a way to die, pretending you have a change of heart. Why don't you ask King Jesus over here to pardon you? He's a king. He can do it."

This made some of the Romans and religious leaders laugh. Marcus, however, did not think Ehud was funny. He simply looked at the prisoner and said, "Do you ever shut up? Your parents should've named you Gestas. Nothing but moans from you. I'd punch you in the gut again, but I think your day is full of enough trouble."

This quieted Ehud for a moment. But not for long.

The time came for the three prisoners to be nailed to their crosses. Marcus and another officer handled Ehud and Micah. As much as Ehud annoyed Marcus, it was still difficult to listen to his cries of pain. The crowd gasped and gawked at the spectacle of gruesome violence before them.

When it was time for Jesus to be nailed to his cross, Longinus ordered one of his new soldiers to do it.

The young man, just old enough to be called such, steadied the first nine-inch iron nail above the wrist of Jesus and raised the hammer. Both of the soldier's hands began to shake.

"What's the problem?" asked Longinus.

"I...I," the soldier stuttered. "I've never done this before."

"It gets easier every time. Pretty soon you won't even think about it."

"No," Jesus said.

Longinus and the young soldier looked at the Nazarene, both surprised he said anything at all.

"What do you mean, *no*?" asked Longinus.

"This is *your* job," said Jesus. "Not his. You do it."

Longinus felt a surge of anger and frustration rising within him.

Deep despair flooded every fiber of his being. He wasn't sure where it came from.

"He has to learn," Longinus said.

"You do it," Jesus reiterated.

Longinus was not used to a prisoner giving him orders or instructions, let alone one about to be executed. He was used to begging, pleading, and bargaining for mercy. Not only was he not able to rescue Jesus, which he felt was the very least he should do in return for once saving Kezia, but now he was forced to take part in his execution. Whether the young soldier nailed Jesus to the cross or not, Longinus was part of this. There was no escaping it. Taking a lesser role did not release him. There would be no washing of hands to transfer guilt to another, as Pilate pretended to do earlier.

Longinus wanted to pray for strength, but to who? Hercules? His ancestors? The only person he ever felt gave him strength was Kezia. He tried to visualize her face in his mind's eye. He whispered a prayer to her and hoped she heard.

He knew an apology to Jesus would be a worthless gesture, but he did so nonetheless.

"For this reason, I've come into the world," said Jesus.

Then Longinus grabbed the nail and hammer from the young soldier and told him to stand back and watch. The centurion tilted his head to focus with his one good eye. He steadied the nail above the wrist and raised the hammer. His heart began to beat faster. Jesus shut his eyes tight and braced himself for the pain.

When all three prisoners were fastened to the wood, the crosses were set in their appropriate holes in the ground. Jesus was the last of the three to be erected, with Micah to his right, and Ehud to his left.

"You said you'd destroy the temple and in three days build it back up," said Annas, staring up at Jesus. "Look at you now."

"Come down from the cross," taunted Theophilus. "Let's talk this over."

"If you are the Son of God, the Chosen One," added Caiaphas, "then save yourself!"

It Is Finished

Just then Caleb and Dinah, led by the twins, Alexander and Rufus, came rushing to the scene of carnage to look for Simon. They called his name.

Simon was fixated on Jesus. Frozen in time. In his trance-like condition, he didn't notice when his family arrived.

"Brother!" Caleb shouted when he spotted him. "You're here. You're alright." Caleb patted Simon's face and body to make sure. "The boys told me they threatened to kill you and then forced you to carry a cross." He spat on the ground as a sign of protest against the Romans. A bit dazed, Simon looked at his brother as if he were only an apparition. It was his wife's voice that snapped him back into reality.

"Simon," she said, then touched his cheek. He looked at Dinah like she was a stranger and began to weep. She wept as well and they embraced.

"Brother, what have they done to you?" asked Caleb. "I'll send word to Caesar if I have to. If Pilate wants to pretend he has no master, we will remind him how very wrong he is."

"Caleb," said Simon. "I'm alright." He hugged his brother.

Caleb calmed down and finally looked at all three faces of the prisoners.

"Are those the two that—"

"They are," Simon interjected before Caleb could finish his question.

"I hope it was worth it, you two!" Caleb shouted at the thieves. He then spat on the ground toward them.

"Brother," said Simon. "Let them be. They are at the end of their lives. They're paying for their sins. Why add to their misery?"

"Why add to their misery?" Caleb repeated. "Did you forget that man held a dagger to Joanna's throat and stole our money? Which, by the way, has not been returned to us from yet even worse thieves." He spat toward the Romans again.

"I have not forgotten," Simon answered.

"Nor have I. So I think a little added misery is in order. Who's the other man?"

"Jesus of Nazareth."

Caleb gasped.

"Look at the sign over his head," said Caiaphas, standing nearby with Annas and some of the other council members. "Did you realize he was our king, Caleb? Should we all bow down at this point? Pilate will pay for that one."

"Caiaphas, old friend," said Caleb, delighted to see him. "What are you doing here?" He went over to speak with the chief priest, whom he had known since he was a child. Simon and Dinah sent the twins back to help Leah. They, however, stayed where they were, holding one another and looking at Jesus, suspended in the air with the sun shining behind him. Dinah did her best to not look at Micah. The loyals of the high priest continued to mock Jesus. They told him to save himself and thus prove he was the Son of God.

"Let this Christ, this king of Israel, come down from the cross," they said. "That's all it will take for us to believe."

"Father, forgive them," Jesus said, looking down at the crowd. "For they do not know what they're doing."

Four of the Roman soldiers joined in the mockery, even bowing down. They divided Jesus's clothing and sandals into four shares and cast lots for the last piece.

"Cut the nonsense," said Longinus, "or I'll have all four of you flogged when we get back."

The soldiers did not understand why their general was so angry. They didn't need to understand. They shut their mouths after that.

"Hey Jesus," said Ehud. "Can you please do me a favor? Can you order our immediate release? I have a very important meeting to attend in a couple of hours. Surely, you—being the king and all—can make this happen. Aren't you the Christ?"

Jesus did not respond to this but Micah did.

"Ehud, enough already!" he said. "Do you not fear God at all? We are getting what we deserve. But this man is innocent. He's done nothing wrong." Micah paused for a moment, then said, "Jesus, please remember me when you come into your kingdom."

Jesus smiled and said, "Great is your faith, Micah. I tell you the truth, today you will be with me in paradise."

Simon could not believe his ears. He watched and listened to this exchange. He clung to every single word that came from the mouth of Jesus. He thought it was fairly righteous of him to stop Caleb from hurling insults at the dying men who robbed them only days earlier. But now he saw the gesture was not enough. Simon somehow knew he needed to forgive the man who held a dagger to his daughter's throat.

But why, Lord? he prayed in his heart. *He's already being punished. What does it matter how I feel about him? My forgiveness will not release him.* Just then, a gentle breeze came through and with it a still small voice. It was not audible. Still, Simon understood it to say that forgiveness will release *him*, not his enemies.

"Mother, why have you come?" said Micah. "I don't want you to see me like this." He hung his head in shame.

Simon looked and noticed a tiny, frail woman, weeping and gazing up at her son. It was Hannah, Micah's mother.

"It's over," Micah said. "I'm so sorry for all I've put you through. Take what I've given you and move from the Lower City. Live a better life."

"I've already gotten rid of it," replied Hannah through her tears. "The money was not given to you and so it should not have been given to me. I'm sorry, son. I know you wanted me to have it. But it wasn't right." Micah looked away.

Simon heard all of this. He looked over to his brother, hoping he did not hear it as well. But Caleb and Caiaphas were in the middle of a deep conversation, which was only interrupted every few moments when the chief priest realized he hadn't shouted an insult at Jesus for a while.

"You must be thrilled," said Ehud. "Your mommy has come. You can now die in peace."

"It's more than I can say for you," said Micah.

To this, Ehud only responded, "I've reaped what I've sown. I won't pretend otherwise. But I will die like a man."

Then Simon saw another distraught woman arrive, led by a

man. Jesus greeted them and told the man he was to be her new son and she his mother.

When Caleb finished talking with Caiaphas, he came back over to tell Simon he was leaving and that he should come back with him.

"I'm going to stay for a bit," said Simon. "Dinah, why don't you go back with Caleb? I'll come soon enough."

Dinah agreed and Caleb spat once again toward the thieves and then toward the Romans before leaving.

Some mocked, some mourned, some stayed, and some left. Simon ignored them all. He simply stood there, staring at Jesus. Longinus and Marcus spoke very little to one another. Soon darkness fell upon the land as though it were night. The people looked up at the sky to search for the sun but could not find it.

Jesus had been quiet for some time before he finally shouted, "It is finished!" He then fell silent and his head dropped to his chest. Jesus of Nazareth was dead. The ground began to shake. The rocks on the cliff of Golgotha started to break and fall from their place. The mourners and onlookers, the Romans, the loyals, members of the Sanhedrin, and the Council of Thirteen began tripping over one another as they lost their balance. In the Praetorium, Pilate's bowl of grapes fell to the floor when the earth quaked beneath him. The walls cracked a bit. The whole city was terrified and wondered what it all meant.

Longinus stayed close to the ground until the trembling stopped. Simon dropped to his knees in worship. Then a hush swept through the land in a breeze. The sun reappeared. People slowly rose to their feet, all a bit apprehensive to do so.

Everything had settled and people felt comfortable to move around again. Ehud and Micah were still managing to breathe by pushing up with their heels against the wooden stump under their feet. Caiaphas approached Marcus and reminded him that because the Sabbath would soon begin, they needed to speed up the death process. All of the prisoners' legs must be broken and their bodies removed from the crosses.

Hannah could not bear to watch her son's legs be broken. She blew a kiss to Micah and said goodbye. Then she hurried away, weeping bitterly. Simon watched Hannah. He suddenly realized she was the very widow from the temple whom Jesus said gave more than everyone else. Simon waited till Hannah was far enough not to notice. Then he followed her back to the shambles she called home in the Lower City.

When Marcus was about to break the legs of Jesus, Longinus stopped him.

"He's already dead," he said. "There's no need."

"I'd feel much more comfortable if you broke his legs," said Caiaphas, who overheard the two Romans talking. "Just to make sure."

"You want proof that he's dead?" asked Longinus. His tone, stature, and grotesque eye frightened the chief priest. Agitated at the request, Longinus took his lance and thrust it into the side of Jesus. Blood and water sprayed from the open flesh and splashed upon the centurion's ruined eye. There was a shooting pain, then everything went black. Longinus collapsed to the ground.

The centurion found himself somewhere between life and death. The world around him disappeared. He was suspended in a void and saw a figure of light walking toward him. It was Kezia. She looked down upon his face and kissed his eye.

"Thank you for your love," she said. "Take good care of our boy now. Give him the best life you know how."

He wrapped his arms around her. Kezia never felt more real to him. Then she caressed his face and said, "Let me go."

A few moments passed and Longinus woke up. He was on his back, staring at the sky. His fellow Romans stood over him.

"Are you alright?" asked Marcus. "Your eye! Look at his eye!"

Longinus blinked and realized he could see perfectly from both eyes. Not only that, but even his flesh was restored. There was no wound or scar. Longinus was healed. He stood to his feet and looked up at the body of Jesus, still hanging on the cross.

"So it's true," he said. "Surely, he *was* the Son of God!"

Then Longinus looked up at the sky and screamed at the top of his lungs, "Barabbas!" He unsheathed his gladius and stabbed it into the earth. Then he took out his dagger and started running.

"Where's he going?" a soldier asked.

"To kill Barabbas," said Marcus. "Let's go watch."

Sweet Revenge

There was a procession of Roman soldiers running behind Longinus, excited to see their general kill a man. Some stayed behind to guard the dead bodies of the prisoners and order the crowd to disperse.

With dagger in hand, Longinus ran from Golgotha to the governor's palace. He was filled with emotions he couldn't describe if he wanted to. Not only could he see from both eyes again, but his vision was somehow sharper.

Finally, he made it to the Praetorium's stables, where the soldier whom he ordered to follow Barabbas was waiting for him with information.

"Where is he?" Longinus asked.

The soldier told him and Longinus took off in that direction, the Roman procession following close behind.

Barabbas was outside his home with his wife and children. He was still basking in the joy of his second chance at life. He felt like a resurrected man. The old Barabbas was dead. He was a new version of himself.

The grateful family sat near the stump of a tree, enjoying the weather of the day. Earlier, he and his wife Deborah had walked out of their home and wondered about the darkness that covered the earth. They gathered their children and held them tight as the whole world shook, wondering if the end of everything had come upon them. Barabbas had no idea what it all meant but thought it might've had something to do with Jesus. Then the chaos ended and the sun returned. Barabbas was a bit like the earth, itself, shaking and full of darkness but now renewed.

He was leaning against the tree when he heard Longinus shout his name. Barabbas turned to the shout's direction and saw a company of Roman soldiers a mere twenty feet away. Standing in front of them in the center was the enormous centurion who had vowed earlier that day to execute him if Pilate did not. Barabbas gulped air. All feelings of newfound gratitude fled from his heart and were promptly replaced with dread.

Longinus raised the dagger in the air and focused on Barabbas with his two perfect eyes.

"Watch this," Marcus said to the soldier next to him. Then he leaned over to Longinus and whispered, "One hundred. Here it comes. Sweet Revenge."

The dagger was released. Barabbas barely had time for his fear to fully settle in. He heard the thud of the dagger when the back of his head banged against the tree. Blood trickled down his face. His wife and children screamed. Barabbas was not sure if he was dead. *Is this what death feels like?* It wasn't much different from being alive. Slowly, Barabbas lifted his hands to the top of his head. He touched the hilt of the dagger that had pinned some of his hair strands to the tree. His wife then ripped her husband's hair from the dagger and frantically examined the wound. The dagger had only grazed his scalp. Nothing more. She wept and laughed at the same time. Barabbas did the same. Then he looked at Longinus and bowed his head slightly as if to say *thank you*. Longinus returned the gesture and walked away.

"You missed," said Marcus to his mentor. "I can't believe you missed. Have you gone blind in both eyes? Where are you going? Try again. This is an easy target. Everyone will mock you as the centurion who can't throw a dagger. You don't want that, do you?"

Longinus did not answer. He kept walking.

"At least let *me* try," insisted Marcus.

"Leave him be," said Longinus.

Marcus hurried to catch up to the general. The company of disappointed soldiers marched behind them.

When Marcus caught up, he asked, "You missed on purpose, didn't you? Tell the truth. You would never miss a mark like that. No way."

Once again, Longinus did not answer.

"At least tell me where you're going."

"Back to Pilate," said Longinus. "I'm resigning."

"You're not serious."

"I am. I can't live with myself."

"That's unfortunate," Marcus said. "There's no one else for you to live with. You know what will happen? What Pilate can do to you? Have you considered that? He'll reduce you to nothing. You'll be taking orders like a servant somewhere."

"I haven't considered anything. All I know is that an innocent man has died. A man powerful enough to restore sight to the blind. Who knows how many other stories about him are true?"

"What do you mean, *restore sight*?" Marcus asked. "I just thought your scar was somehow gone. Are you telling me you can see again?"

Longinus stopped to show Marcus his healed eye.

"Prove it," Marcus said. "Close your other eye and tell me how many fingers I'm holding up."

Longinus did so and got the answer right.

"What about now?" Marcus said.

Once again, Longinus answered correctly.

"Maybe your eye was swollen and you weren't truly blind," said Marcus.

Longinus continued walking and said, "A blade went through my eye, Marcus. The doctor sealed the wound with a burning hawthorn stick. My eye was still ruined when I woke up this morning."

"It's a curious thing," said Marcus. "I'll give you that."

"Besides, I don't care what Pilate does," said Longinus. "He has no real power. He's a puppet like the rest of them. He can't do anything to me."

"Have you not met Pontius Pilate? Remind me to introduce you to him later. He's simply lovely."

"That's not what I mean, Marcus. If I don't care about whatever disciplinary actions he takes, then he has no power over me. Now I want you to do something. Please pay attention."

"Anything," answered Marcus.

"There's an innkeeper named Nathan who lives two miles away from the city. Tonight, I want you to bring my son to him. He will be his father now." Longinus gave Marcus directions to the inn from the governor's palace.

"But you are his father," said Marcus. "*You* should take care of him. The boy wants to be like you. That much is obvious. You'll probably only be fined. You've served well. I don't think you have much to worry about. Forget what I said before. And where will you be, that I should have to take your son anywhere? Pilate won't arrest you for resigning prematurely. You told me you wanted to do it anyway. It's not a crime. Shameful, sure. But not a crime."

"I am the last thing I want my son to be like. Just remember what I said. Can you do that for me?"

"I'll remember."

Marcus was confused but wanted to honor his mentor's wishes. He asked no more questions.

Resignation

Most of the other soldiers dispersed when Longinus arrived back at the palace. Marcus and a few others followed him to where Pilate sat, still eating his grapes and drinking his wine. They waited for Pilate to finish speaking with two prominent Pharisees. Joseph of Arimathea was requesting to take the body of Jesus to be placed in a tomb he had cut into a small rocky hill on his property. Standing close behind him with his head held high was Nicodemus.

"The Nazarene's body?" Pilate asked.

"He has died, Governor," said Joseph. "I was there when it happened."

"Dead already?" Pilate then noticed Longinus and Marcus standing nearby. "Is this true?"

"It is," Longinus said. "We broke the legs of the two thieves, but the Nazarene was already dead before this."

"Interesting," Pilate said. "Does Caiaphas know you want to give this man a proper burial? He won't approve. He may want me to burn him like a prisoner without family. Are you not afraid of getting caught with a different opinion from the high priest? Heaven forbid!"

Nicodemus scoffed at the idea, for he no longer feared the high priest. This reaction amused Pilate.

"The Sabbath is approaching," said Joseph. "It's unclean to have bodies hanging in public. I'm friends with the Nazarene's mother and intend to honor her son. I have to do what's right in the sight of God, whether the high priest likes it or not."

"I like you, Joseph," said Pilate. "If giving the Nazarene a proper burial will annoy Caiaphas, then I say let's do it! Guards, escort these two men to Golgotha. Assist them in removing the Nazarene from the cross and allow them to take the body. Remove the thieves as well."

Joseph and Nicodemus thanked the governor and left the palace with two guards. Pilate continued with his grapes and wine. He noticed Longinus and Marcus had not left.

"Do you need something from me?" he asked. "Why are you still here?"

Longinus laid down his shield, his lance, and a few other items at the governor's feet.

"What are you doing?" Pilate asked.

"Though it has been my life's honor," Longinus began, "I'm terminating my service in the Roman army, effective immediately."

"*You* want to terminate your service? That's funny. I didn't realize it was *your* decision to do so. How long has it been, anyway?"

"A bit over over ten years, sir."

"Ten years," Pilate repeated. "An incomplete career. Not to mention a complete desertion of your stately duties. Where's your patriotism?"

Pilate stared at the centurion for a moment and popped a grape in his mouth. Then he sipped his wine. Then he ate a few more grapes. He stared at some of the new cracks in the wall from the earthquake earlier.

"Resign," he muttered. "Men generally don't resign from the Roman army. They complete their time of service and retire with honor and dignity. You've obviously risen through the ranks. Not everyone gets promoted to centurion. What's your name again?"

"Longinus."

"A terrible name. Ten years you say? It takes at least that amount of time to even become a centurion. Usually longer. How long have you been one?"

"About five years."

"Half the time than most. Only the best men can achieve such a high rank in such a short amount of time. Why do you wish to give this up?"

"He healed me, sir."

"Healed you? Who healed you?"

"Jesus."

"Jesus? Which one? The whore killer I released or the one you just crucified?"

Longinus felt a sharp pain in his chest. Though he wasn't sure if it was for nailing Jesus to the cross, how close he came to vengefully killing Barabbas, or how flippantly Pilate called Kezia a whore. Perhaps all three mingled into one like an unholy trinity of regret, guilt, and shame.

"The latter, sir," Longinus managed to answer with an increasingly shaky voice.

Pilate looked visibly agitated.

"And what did he heal you from?" he asked. "Surely not your insanity."

A few of Pilate's private guards laughed at this until Pilate silenced them with a look of admonishment.

"My left eye, sir. You remember it was wounded in the insurrection? I was completely blinded by Silvanus's dagger."

"What, that scratch you showed me? Oh, thank heavens. Now I can sleep again, knowing you will survive. Shall I prepare a feast to celebrate?"

The guards chuckled once more until Pilate turned sharply toward their direction. They were not to laugh again.

"So tell me," Pilate continued, annoyed and almost bored. "How did a dying man magically heal your eye?"

Longinus stuttered, searching for the right way to describe what happened. He kept it simple and told him everything he remembered.

"So you're telling me," said Pilate, "you pierced his side, and the fluid that came out of the wound landed on your eye and healed it? Is that about right?"

"Exactly."

"I see...and now *you*—apparently—see, as well." Pilate laughed at his own joke and turned to his guards, hoping to find them laughing as well, but they were like stone statues with blank stares.

"It was a joke," Pilate said. "Laugh!"

The guards began laughing hysterically on command.

"That's enough," he said. He bent down to examine the items on the floor. "So this is the lance that pierced the side that healed you?" Pilate picked it up and studied it closely. "Guards, bring this to my wife. I shall keep it for my private collection." Then something visibly bothered him. He looked at the remaining items, then back up at Longinus. Something was missing. "Where is your gladius?"

Longinus bowed his head and said, "I left it where it belongs, sir...at the feet of Jesus."

"Did we not have nails for that?"

"We did. I stabbed the sword into the ground."

"Of course you did. Why? Did the ground attack you or something?"

Longinus suddenly realized where he was and to whom he was speaking. But there was no backing out now. He'd face whatever consequence came, like the warrior he was. He responded with, "My sword is stained with the blood of a hundred men. Well... almost a hundred men."

"And it will be stained with the blood of a hundred more," Pilate said, "whether *you* wield it or not. That's what swords are for. Are you in need of basic training again? *At the feet of Jesus...*" He mumbled the last part to himself before shouting, "Do dead men require weaponry? It's a little too late for Jesus to pick up the sword now, is it not? And where on earth is your dagger? Also with Jesus?"

"That's with the other Jesus," answered Longinus.

"Why am I not surprised? I'm sure you have a great story for this one. I would love to hear it."

"I threw it at his head."

"Then you have finally said something I don't find utterly repulsive," Pilate said. "And where is the body of Barabbas?"

"The dagger missed, sir. Barabbas lives. It only grazed his scalp and landed on the tree behind him near his home. Not far from here."

"So not only are you a quitter, but you're also growing incompetent. Perhaps it *is* time for you to step down. Or did you miss on purpose? Listen carefully. I don't know what kind of sorcery this poor and—may I remind you—very dead rabbi was capable of, but I'm growing quite weary of hearing about it. Magical or not, he's gone. Like the wind, gone; like my first wife, gone; like Alexander of Macedon, gone; like the two thieves crucified next to him, gone. Need I continue? Great or not so great, he's dead. You're disrupting your entire life for a mortal. Someone like you and me."

"He was an innocent man," Longinus interjected.

"There's no such thing," Pilate said. He stood to his feet, popped a grape in his mouth, and began pacing. "So what if he did not deserve to die? If I spared his life today, would he not die tomorrow or some other day? What's the difference? Should I have let him live to make this city crazier than it already is? How dare you criticize my decision! I should kill you for that. Right here. Right now. I should cut your head off and put it on a stake, then stick it outside for every centurion, decurion, and legionary in my army to see what I think of delusional quitters who criticize me. I'd use your blood for ink and write a sign that reads—what's your name again?"

"Longinus."

"Longinus! Yes! It would read, 'Longinus, The Incompetent and Delusional.' And then maybe in small print, 'Got what he deserved!' Or something to that effect. Maybe I'd even stick my hand through your neck hole to operate your mouth and make you say, *'I'm a quitter! I'm a quitter!'* Despicable! Simply despicable! Do you have a replacement? Or do you expect *me* to step down and do *your* job? For the love of all that is sacred, take care to answer wisely."

Pontius Pilate sat back down in his chair. His grape bowl was empty and so was his wine cup. He told his servant to fetch him more of both. Then Pilate glared at his subordinate and waited for a reply.

"But of course," Longinus said. "I've been training Marcus here for almost a year now."

Marcus was off to the side, watching this whole ordeal unfold. His mouth dropped. He stepped forward at the mention of his name. Pilate looked him up and down and took notice of his rank.

"A decurion," the governor said. "Can he handle a bigger load? More than double his current squadron?"

"Marcus has proven himself in every regard," said Longinus. "His soldiers respect and obey him. He is a master swordsman. He is disciplined and shows restraint when needed and is not afraid to punish. In my opinion, his current load is too light for such a qualified man."

"Have you trained him to be a quitter as well?" Pilate asked.

"No, Governor. You won't find a more loyal replacement."

Pilate nodded along, as he considered the recommendation.

"Very well," he said. Then turning to Marcus, "Your very first assignment is to fetch me the gladius of—what on earth is your name again?"

"Longinus."

"Longinus, yes. Hopefully, a peasant hasn't already snatched it up to start the next pathetic revolt against us. Step forward, please."

Longinus stepped forward.

"Closer," Pilate said.

With caution, Longinus stepped forward once more.

"Closer," Pilate said.

Longinus obeyed.

"Close enough for me to whisper in your ear."

Longinus braced himself for cruelty. A biting off of his earlobe, perhaps. A knife to his side. Something sudden and torturous. He wasn't sure if he'd be able to contain a violent response. But instead, Pilate did whisper in his ear.

"Your attire belongs to a decorated general. Take off that ridiculous costume. No need to pretend anymore. You are no longer a centurion."

Longinus stripped down till he was almost naked, save his loin cloth.

"However," Pilate continued. "Your service in the Roman military has not been terminated. You'll pay the standard fine for quitters and work in the armory for the duration of your career. The training for your demotion starts tomorrow. Understand?"

Longinus nodded in disappointment. He feared Pilate would react in such an anticlimactic manner. But before he had the chance to be dismissed, the ex-centurion said, "One more thing."

"Yes?" said Pilate with a sigh of exasperation.

"Silvanus did not betray you. I did. Silvanus fought me when he realized it, but I prevailed against him."

Pontius Pilate was stunned at the confession. Marcus's mouth dropped once again.

"Governor, that isn't true," Marcus interjected at once.

Pilate raised his hand to silence the new centurion. Then he rose from his chair again and stood directly in front of Longinus.

"Why would you make such a confession?" he asked. "You did not have to. Why now? You only received a demotion and a fine. Then in a single swift and foolish moment, you go from quitter to traitor. Is that what you're telling me? That you had something to do with the insurrection?"

"I helped organize it. I gave rebels Roman military attire and gave the signal for the attack. I helped plot it. I am not fit to live."

Pilate looked into his eyes.

"This changes everything, doesn't it?" he said. "It doesn't even matter if it's true or not. You confessed you are guilty of treason. Now I must act." Then he shouted into the air, "What is taking so long with my grapes and wine?"

A servant came running in with a fresh supply of grapes and a bottle of new wine. Pontius Pilate sat back down. He sipped the wine and popped a grape in his mouth.

"I truly don't feel like going out to the Stone Pavement right now," the governor said. "And I do not wish to execute anyone."

Marcus breathed a sigh of relief.

"But the law is the law," he continued. "I don't write the rules, I just enforce them. Guards, put this man in the pit. Find a solitary cell that is separate from the other insurrectionists. You, new guy. What's your name again?"

"Marcus, sir."

"Marcus, there's been enough bloodshed for one day. You will lead the execution of your mentor first thing tomorrow morning. If you have a problem with this, you can join him. Any questions?"

"No, sir," replied Marcus.

"Good. When it's done, report back to me before I finish breakfast. Someone fetch me papyrus and meet me at the judgment seat outside. I'll sign the execution order at once."

Pilate's private guards began placing Longinus in chains.

"I will be number one hundred," Longinus told Marcus, as he was being led out of Pilate's presence. "Remember what I said about my son. Bring him to Nathan, the innkeeper. He'll take good care of him, I'm sure of it. I told you where he lives."

"I remember," Marcus said. The newly appointed centurion could not figure out what was going through his mentor's mind. Perhaps he went mad right before his eyes. Marcus looked on in bewilderment and horror masked as indifference, as it was the first time he had ever seen Longinus look so utterly powerless.

Paradise

Hannah collapsed at her threshold and wailed. Her neighbor Ruth ran out to console her.

Simon was overwhelmed with conflicting emotions, as he looked on from around a corner. He wanted to continue hating the man who had put a dagger to his daughter's throat. But Micah's mother seemed so human, so powerless, so very normal. It struck Simon that all three of his children were still alive, while this woman's only son was not.

Then he looked at the surroundings. He never had a reason to visit the Lower City before. The homes were made of mud bricks and rotting wood. Many roofs were about to collapse. Dirty half-naked children begged wealthier strangers for bread and coins. Simon imagined Micah was probably one of them when he was young.

"I couldn't do it, Ruth," said Hannah. "I couldn't watch them do it. I couldn't stay there to see my son die. He needed me there. But I left."

"Oh, Hannah. I'm sure he wouldn't want his mother watching it," said Ruth. "You did the right thing."

"And now what will become of his body? My only son's body? Those brutes will burn him. Desecrate him."

Hearing these words, Simon suddenly became indignant. He left at once to visit Pontius Pilate.

Boldly, he demanded to speak with the governor when he arrived at the palace. He had practiced everything he was to say on the way over.

Just because this criminal's mother is a poor widow does not mean she doesn't deserve to bury her dead. This is no way to treat the residents of this city. You are fully aware that we Jews do not burn our dead. We bury them.

But much of this bold speech was to be left out. Pilate could not care less about Micah's body.

"Take it," he said. "Take the other thief's body while you're at it. Why should I care?"

Simon had no interest in taking Ehud's body and left it for the Romans to burn with the other unclaimed corpses from the pit.

Simon was not a very strong man, but when the Roman soldier placed Micah's body in his arms, he was determined to carry it all the way from Golgotha to Hannah's humble home in the Lower City.

People stared at the rich man struggling to not drop a bloody dead criminal and reasoned they must've been related. Simon began to weep for Micah. He no longer saw him as the violent thief who stole from his brother, killed the guards, and threatened his daughter's life. He was simply the only son of a poor and helpless widow—a son whose life was now lost.

Simon came to Hannah's threshold and gently placed Micah on the ground. Hannah was inside with Ruth when he arrived. She stood to her feet at the sight.

"Micah?" she said. "You brought my son! You brought my son to me!"

Hannah fell to her knees and embraced Micah, weeping over him.

"But who are you?"

"My name is Simon."

Hannah kissed Micah on his forehead.

"Where shall I bury him?" she asked.

"I have the perfect place," said Simon. "But you must wrap him and prepare his body before I take you there."

"I don't have the means," said Hannah.

"I'll help you," said Ruth. "The Lord has recently given me more money than I know what to do with. I'll pay any neighbor who has something to offer."

People came out of their homes and got involved as well. With a little from here and a little from there, Micah's body was anointed with oils and perfume and then wrapped in strips of linen. Hannah kissed her son before they bound the face covering to his head. A man from a few dilapidated homes away came with a cot to place Micah on and offered to help carry him to the burial site. Simon lifted the cot from the other side. He led the small procession of poor mourners to Caleb's garden.

The sun was setting, and along the way, they walked past a centurion by the name of Cornelius.

"Buried at sunset," Cornelius said to the group of mourners. "How beautiful! I don't know who this man is, but I shall give this individual the name Dismas."

Cornelius said a prayer for Micah and blessed Hannah. Simon couldn't help but think of how different this Roman was from all the rest. Surely, the Lord is doing a new thing, he thought.

Caleb and Leah, along with Dinah and the children came running out to meet Simon and the strangers he came with.

"Brother, what is going on?" Caleb said. "There's blood all over you. What happened? Who are these people? Who is *that*?" He looked at the wrapped body lying on the cot.

"Caleb," said Simon, "I'm fine. These are friends."

"Friends?" Caleb asked incredulously. Then he whispered in Simon's ear, "How could this be? They are all so very poor. How could they be friends of yours?"

"This man was struck down in the prime of his life. I would like to honor him and his mother with a proper burial." Simon looked in the direction of the tombs Caleb had shown him just days earlier.

Understanding what his brother meant, Caleb said, "You're not suggesting we put this man where the family is supposed to be buried?"

"There's more than enough room," said Simon.

"But who is this man?" asked Caleb. "He's not family."

Simon took his brother to the side to speak privately with him.

"Brother, I know this is hard for you," he began. "But these people are my good friends. If I were back home in Cyrene, I'd bury him as one of my own. But his mother lives here in Jerusalem. It wouldn't be fair of me to take her son away from her like that."

"You never answered my question," said Caleb. "How do you know these people, let alone call them your friends, even going as far as to suggest they are like family? Oh, I get it. This is some type of charity. Is this something that Jesus criminal put you up to?"

"No, these are my friends. Believe it or not. If you want to think of it as charity, go ahead. I am no longer restricting my associations to the rich only. The dead man and his mother are friends of mine. And Jesus was no criminal."

Just then, Dinah came up to them and said, "Simon, who are these people?"

But Caleb did not let his brother answer. "Doesn't matter, Dinah. They are friends of your husband in need of a proper burial. Go ahead, brother. I will allow it. But don't make this a public space. This is my home, after all."

Simon smiled and embraced Caleb. Dinah tugged on her husband's arm to get his attention. Ever so discreetly, he whispered in her ear, "I'll tell you later, my love." They walked back to the small group of mourners and led them to the garden tombs.

Hannah and the neighbors who accompanied her tore their garments and wept. They blessed the Lord and prayed for peace. Micah's body was placed in one of Caleb's family tombs and a stone was rolled over the entrance. When Caleb was officially introduced to Hannah, he told her she could visit whenever she wanted.

One by one, the mourners left. Simon walked Hannah to the property gate.

"It's like a private paradise over here," Hannah said. "It's more than my son deserves. Much more. He did not live a good life."

"His troubles are over," said Simon. "He's with the Lord now. I'm sure of it."

Hannah smiled and said, "I still don't know who you are, but I thank you. You made a very difficult day for me so much easier to bear."

"What else are friends for?" he said.

Hannah nodded and turned away. Simon watched her catch up to Ruth.

Dinah came up from behind Simon and embraced him.

"The man we buried," Simon began, "I can explain."

But she stopped him from finishing his sentence.

"I already know," Dinah said. "I'm not sure how I feel about it yet. But I do know it was the right thing to do. We should prepare to leave soon."

Following Orders

Late in the night, well before dawn, the young Longinus was still awake. He grew anxious when his father never came back to the room. The physician had come earlier, expecting to examine his father's ruined eye, but the boy told him he never returned. Neither the boy nor the physician knew of the miraculous healing that had taken place.

The young Longinus finally resolved to leave the room and search for his father. But as soon as he put on his sandals, he heard the familiar knock on the door. The boy ran to remove the bar. He was immediately disappointed.

"Your father sent me for you," said Marcus in his broken Aramaic. "We're leaving the city right now. Do you have any belongings to pack?"

"What do you mean?" the boy asked. "Where are we going? Where's my father?"

"He had matters to attend to and so he sent me for you. Now hurry and gather your things."

The boy only had a dagger in his sack. He grabbed pieces of fruit and unleavened bread from the food table to stuff in there as well. Reluctantly, he followed Marcus out of his father's room. He remembered meeting Marcus but was curious as to why he was now dressed as a centurion and asked about it on the way to the stables.

"I've been promoted. Your father has been training me for a while. Pilate has finally accepted the recommendation."

"Congratulations," the boy said. "When will I see my father? Is he meeting up with us?"

Ignoring the questions, Marcus helped the boy onto the horse. Then he mounted his own and began to lead the way out of the city. The boy looked around the dirt road. He was very familiar with the surroundings. It didn't take more than a few minutes for the young Longinus to stop.

"No," he said.

Marcus stopped as well and turned around.

"What do you mean, no?" he asked.

"You're taking me to Nathan."

"It's where your father wants you," Marcus said. "Is Nathan a bad man?"

"No. He taught me many things. But he's not my father and I don't want to go there. You can't force me."

Marcus chuckled at this and said, "I'm a general now. If I can't force a boy like yourself to do something he doesn't want to do then I wouldn't be fit for my new role in Pilate's army."

"Then maybe you're not fit for your new role in Pilate's army."

Marcus liked the young Longinus and could see he already had his father's boldness.

"I'm not going," the boy continued. "And you can't make me because my father is a mighty centurion."

"He also happens to be a mighty idiot," said Marcus.

"What did you just call him? He is much bigger than you. I don't care if you're a centurion now. He's been one for years and still outranks you. You have to answer to him if you hurt me."

Marcus dismounted his horse and walked over to the young Longinus.

"I'm not going to hurt you, boy. I'm following your father's orders by taking you to the innkeeper."

"But why?" he asked. "Why do I have to go back to Nathan's? I want to learn how to be a centurion. I've already lost my mother. I'm not losing my father too. Where is he? I belong with *him*. Not Nathan."

Marcus stared at him for a moment. In addition to his father's boldness and determination, the boy had captivating blue eyes like his mother. Suddenly an idea entered his mind.

"You know what?" Marcus said. "I agree. You do belong with your father. Maybe this will work. I'll need your bag."

"Maybe what will work?"

The boy handed over his bag, as he asked the question. Marcus promptly emptied its contents onto the ground and said, "Keep the food and dagger." He walked back to his horse. After mounting, he turned toward the direction of the city. As Marcus passed the boy he said, "Stay here till I return. Don't go anywhere. Stay off the road and remain in the shadows. I'll be back in a bit. If I don't return before the sun rises, you'll have to go to Nathan's on your own. I'm sure you know your way from here."

"I don't want to go to Nathan's," the boy shouted, watching the new centurion ride away. "Where are you off to?"

Marcus did not answer.

The young Longinus was confused. He wasn't sure if he could trust Marcus but didn't feel he had a choice. He dismounted his horse and looked around. There was a large fig tree on the side of the dirt road. The boy tied his horse to it and stood there, looking up at the stars.

Old Friends

The guard in charge of the armory stood to his feet immediately when he saw the centurion approach.

"I need a few things," said Marcus. "Let me in."

"Of course," the guard responded.

Marcus entered the room full of weaponry, armor, and various supplies. He stuffed a dagger, a pair of military sandals, a large set of linen undergarments, and a tunic into the sack he took from the boy. There was not enough space for the helmet. Marcus then grabbed a decent-sized breastplate. He draped his cloak over these last two items and exited the armory.

Marcus marched directly to the prison commander in charge of the pit and showed him his execution orders.

"I sent an officer down here earlier," Marcus said. "He was to guard the new traitor till his execution."

The prison commander looked at Marcus suspiciously. Then he spat on the ground at the mention of a traitor.

"I'll also be sending the inner prison guards up while I conduct a recount of the rebels."

"A recount?" the commander asked. "I know my guards are not the brightest bunch, but they can count just fine."

"Very well. I'll be sure to let Pilate know of your confidence in them."

The commander snarled slightly at this and said, "Do what you must and be quick about it."

"Of course."

He breathed a sigh of relief. As he descended the dimly lit stone passageway, Marcus felt his heart race, knowing what he was about to do. He prayed it would somehow work. He did everything he could to trick himself into having the authoritative confidence of the general he now was. He took a deep breath before making his final turn.

The two standing guards straightened out their posture immediately at the sight of the new centurion.

"How many?" Marcus asked.

"Forty-seven," one answered with a slight stutter. "Not including the new traitor we put in the solitary cell." All three of them spat on the ground in unison when this was said. "Two prisoners have already been crucified," the guard continued. "One was released. Not sure how many have died recently. We've already removed and disposed of four. Shall I do another count now?"

"No," Marcus answered. "I will conduct my own count. You two leave me be. Consider it a break. I'll come get you when I'm done."

The lead guard handed over the key to the gate that led the way to the inner prison.

"And the keys to the shackles," Marcus said.

The guards looked at one another, not knowing what to do.

"I gave you an order," Marcus reminded them, slowly raising his punishment stick, his heart racing still.

"But...but...sir, we are on strict orders to hold the shackle keys until the end of our shift, then we give them to the next guards. We have no desire to disobey you."

"Then don't," Marcus said sharply. "No one is being released, you idiots. I want to separate the living from the dead."

"Oh, of course. I can do that for you, myself. No trouble at all. It's certainly no job for someone of your rank."

Swiftly, Marcus struck the guard's face with the punishment stick and broke his nose. The other guard straightened up even more so than he already was and said nothing while his friend bled.

"Give me the shackle keys or both of you will have a very bad day today."

The guard with the broken nose motioned to his partner to do as they were told.

"Now go upstairs and wait outside till I'm through with my count," Marcus said in a cold and calm tone. "If I see you down here before I fetch for you, you will pay for the offense in blood."

The frightened and humiliated guards left as quickly as they could. Marcus let out another sigh of relief.

He gently placed the breastplate and helmet on the ground so both of his hands were free. He opened the gates to the inner prison and walked down a small corridor leading to the room holding most of the rebels.

The rancid stench was much worse than when he first entered the pit. It was all Marcus could do to not vomit instantly. He covered his nose with his cape. Rats were scurrying about and feasting on two lifeless bodies.

The shackled prisoners shuttered at the sight of the centurion. Marcus began counting. Forty-seven was accurate, including the two deceased prisoners being eaten by rats. How many else were dead, he couldn't tell.

"Don't torture us, please!" one begged.

"I haven't come to torture anyone," Marcus said, muffled through the forearm and cloak still covering his nose. "Anyone else dead besides these two rat meals?"

"That fellow at the end," a prisoner offered. "He was a lot more talkative yesterday." The chained man did his best to nod in the direction with his head.

Marcus walked over to the body. The stature was a good match but he was circumcised. Marcus couldn't be careless with details. He then proceeded to poke every prisoner who looked unresponsive. Some woke up in horror at the sight of him. One did not wake up at all. But he too was circumcised and therefore of no use.

There was no other choice. Marcus placed one hand over his heart, which was quickly filling up with dread. He was cold and numb. He approached Felix slowly and swallowed hard when he saw his face.

"Felix, is that you, old friend?"

"Marcus," Felix whispered painfully. "You're a centurion now. Congratulations."

"What happened to your face? Your nose and lips look wretched."

Struggling to get the words out, Felix answered, "Some of my soldiers visited yesterday. I guess they learned I was a traitor. I was never very kind to them."

Aside from a swollen face beyond recognition, Felix was not doing well otherwise. Marcus had ordered the physician to check on him every day, whether he accompanied him or not. But some wounds run too deep and can't be healed. He was soaked in sweat. His fever and infected injuries had all but taken his life.

"Always the strong one," Marcus said. They shared a moment of silence. Marcus finally broke it with a memory. "Do you remember back home, a long time ago when we were—I don't know—maybe twelve years of age? Your mother caught me stealing your father's bow and quiver."

Marcus began to chuckle at the memory and continued.

"I froze as if death itself had tapped my shoulder. She tugged on my ear so hard I thought it would rip right off. I remember being so relieved it was she who caught me and not your father. She was the more merciful of the two. Do you remember that, Felix?"

"I do," he whispered. "Why do you think I gave you his bow and quiver when he died? Surely they meant more to you than me."

It hurt Felix to laugh but he did so nonetheless.

"My mother never stopped referring to you as my *thief-friend*," said Felix. "Even up to the day we left to be added to Pilate's numbers. She asked if I was sure I wanted to travel with a criminal."

"Very unforgiving, that mother of yours," said Marcus.

"She was, indeed."

The two friends reminisced a bit more. They kept their voices down, though the other prisoners were too exhausted to care about the exchange. There was a moment when neither uttered a word. Marcus looked at Felix with a feigned smile.

"Do what you've come to do," said Felix.

Marcus was surprised by his friend's intuition.

"I don't want to," he said.

"But you must. It would be an act of mercy. Believe me. This is no way to finish my life. If my injuries don't kill me by tomorrow, my men will come back and do worse and you know it. It hurts to even talk."

Marcus nodded. It was true.

"Very well," he sighed. "Let's get this over with. Are you ready, old friend?"

"I am," replied Felix.

"Travel well."

Felix closed his swollen eyes and waited. Marcus gulped air and held it till the deed was done. With one quick and forceful maneuver, Marcus thrust his dagger into Felix's heart, then twisted the blade to hasten the process.

Felix faced his death bravely. Grateful even.

Marcus removed the dagger from Felix's chest and cleaned the blade before sheathing it. He placed his dagger-thrusting hand gently on his friend's shoulder and waited for him to die. It did not take long. The pit was quiet. One prisoner who saw what happened began to whimper, thinking the centurion would make his rounds and start killing them all off.

"Hush now," Marcus said to him. "Today is not your day."

He then released Felix from his chains. He put his arms under Felix's and used the punishment stick to assist in the dragging.

Marcus dropped Felix to the floor outside of the inner cell. He then went back and got the two recently deceased prisoners and set them on top of one another next to Felix. He left the two rat-infested bodies alone.

Marcus locked the cell doors. He placed Felix on the large breastplate he took from the armory to prevent a trail of blood. Felix was dragged down long corridors till Marcus finally reached a solitary cell at the end of one. He dropped Felix and opened the cell door.

The Switch

Longinus was naked in a corner, chained to the wall and ground. His mouth and nose were bleeding and he had several lacerations across his chest from whips.

"Marcus," he said, "Have you come to execute me? I'm sorry. I did not think Pilate would order you to do that. Make it quick, please. Let's get on with it."

"I've killed one friend today. I don't need to kill another. What were you thinking, confessing to crimes you didn't commit? Why not just slit your own throat if you wanted to die? Have you lost your mind? Am I about to free a crazy man?"

"Free me? Marcus, no. Pilate will kill you if he finds out."

Marcus found the key to begin unshackling his mentor.

"Pilate won't find out. Dead men lie not. It's their only virtue."

"I don't deserve to live, Marcus. I killed the man who healed my eye and saved the love of my life. Surely he was more than a good man, not worthy of death. I nailed him to the wood, myself."

"Because it was your job. What choice did you have?"

"We always have a choice."

"We don't have time for this. It's almost dawn. Whether you deserve it or not, you've got a second chance at life. The old you is officially dead. Your son needs *you*, not Nathan. We have to hurry."

"My boy, how is he?"

"As stubborn as you," said Marcus. "And certainly not interested in going to the innkeeper."

"Who is this man?" Longinus said, staring at the body near his feet.

"You remember Felix. I introduced you to him on our march up. I've known him since childhood. Does it matter? He was unfortunately a traitor—a real traitor, not a pretend one like you—and now here he is. He's about your size, don't you think?"

Longinus began to understand the plan. He looked at Felix carefully, as his body lay face up on the ground.

"He doesn't look like me, Marcus."

"That's the point. His men bashed his face in yesterday. Or rather it was *I* who bashed in *your* face today. You can now barely tell he's younger than you."

Longinus stood to his feet once he was freed. He stretched out his arms and legs.

"What about the prisoner headcount?" he asked.

"Simple miscount," answered Marcus. Several have died. Easy mistake. The count changes by the day."

Longinus grabbed Marcus by his arm and said, "Are you sure about this? I won't be able to repay you."

Marcus patted his mentor on the shoulder and said, "I took your job. We're even."

Longinus chuckled at this and the two embraced.

"Well, you're the centurion now," said Longinus. "I better do what I'm told. How am I getting out of here?"

Marcus pulled out the sack from under his cloak and emptied the contents he had taken from the armory. Longinus immediately began to put on the undergarments and tunic. He then strapped on the military sandals.

"Not exactly fit for an officer," Marcus said. "But it'll do. Take this dagger and put on the helmet. I also fetched your gladius. Pilate's orders."

Longinus was hoping to never see it again.

"I'm fairly certain he did not want you to give it back to me," he said.

"You're not very good at this, are you? It was already gone when I went to retrieve it. Simple story, right?"

Marcus used some of the tunic to wipe off Felix's blood from the breastplate. "Stay close to me and keep quiet. You'll look the part, no problem."

"You expect me to simply walk out of here?" asked Longinus.

"Either that or be beaten to death and carried out of here. Your choice."

"They may beat both of us to death."

"The risk is mine, not yours."

They chained Felix in place of Longinus. They did their best to clean off more blood from the breastplate his body was dragged on. Longinus put on the helmet that barely fit. Marcus locked the solitary cell. They walked up the stone pathway.

"Remember, stay directly behind me," Marcus whispered, as they approached the backs of the guards still waiting to return to their post.

"Ehem," Marcus coughed to get their attention. The two turned around immediately.

"Did you not tell me there were forty-seven prisoners?" Marcus asked.

The guard with the broken nose said, "I did, sir. I counted them, myself."

"Well, I counted forty-six. That includes four deaths. Two have died recently. I've laid them outside to be collected and properly disposed of. There are two more who have been dead for days and are being eaten by rats, as we speak. I expect you to take care of this at once. Do you understand me?" Marcus raised his stick.

"Right away, sir."

The prison commander rushed over.

"What's all this about?" he asked. "Why are you harassing my guards?" He glanced at Longinus suspiciously, who kept quiet the whole time.

"Your guards have miscounted the prisoners," Marcus said.

"This one told me there were forty-seven, but I counted forty-six in total. Four dead and forty-two still living. This does not include the traitor we just executed, who needs to be disposed of as well. I left him in his cell."

"Alright, alright," the commander said. "Let's calm down. We'll take care of it." He sent his guards back to their post.

Marcus and Longinus proceeded to leave the building.

"One minute," the commander stopped them.

Their hearts froze. They turned around slowly. A storm of nerves raged inside each of them. With a stone face and a glare colder than ice, the commander marched up to Marcus and placed something in his palm.

Marcus looked down at the leather pouch of coins. Very quietly the commander said, "You won't alert the governor of this discrepancy, will you?"

"What discrepancy?" Marcus asked as he took the money.

"Good man," the commander replied. The two friends exited the palace and went to the stables.

The sun was still not up and the city was dark and quiet.

"Where to now?" Longinus asked.

"Not far."

As Marcus led his mentor to the boy, he took the opportunity to ask, "So you truly think that rabbi had some type of magical power or something?"

"I was blind, but now I see, Marcus. How can you explain it without thinking he was some kind of god?"

"Gods don't die."

"I know nothing about the life and death of gods. Only what I experienced."

"I don't know," said Marcus. "Unless a god appeared to me directly, I wouldn't believe such a thing. Certainly not enough to quit this job. So what was your plan? You wanted to cleanse yourself from participating in his execution by allowing *yourself* to be executed?"

"Something like that."

"You should've washed your hands like Pilate. Much less dramatic."

Marcus led his mentor about half a mile away to a horse tied to a tree. The boy turned around when he heard the two men approach.

"Abba!" he cried out.

"Son!" Longinus began to weep, as he grabbed him into his arms. "I thought I'd never see you again."

The boy whispered something into his father's ear.

"Oh, I'm sure Marcus did not mean to call me an idiot?" said Longinus.

"I very much did mean it," said Marcus.

"Aren't you going to punish him?" the boy asked.

"Like father, like son," Marcus said.

"He saved my life," answered Longinus. "I think we can forgive an insult or two."

"Ah, then I have one more to go," said Marcus.

The two friends laughed and the father and boy mounted their horses.

"Take this," Marcus said, handing Longinus the pouch of bribe money he had just received. "I'm sure you can use it for the journey. You may want to take off that helmet and breastplate before leaving. Without an army, Romans tend to look like targets around here."

Longinus removed his breastplate and helmet and threw them near the tree. He handed Marcus his sword.

"No," Marcus said. "This is *your* gladius. It will always be yours."

"I don't want it anymore," Longinus said. "I meant it when I laid it down. I won't be needing it. I'm a citizen of a new kingdom now. A kingdom of peace."

"Treason," Marcus joked. "I should bring you back to the pit this instant. Take the sword and dagger for your travels. You already know bandits prowl the roads all the way to the coast. If not for your own defense, you have a son to protect."

Longinus wanted to be done with violence once and for all. But the thought of protecting his son outweighed his new contempt for bloodshed.

"Fair enough," Longinus said.

The two Romans embraced for the last time and parted ways.

Pilate was almost through with breakfast when Marcus entered his private chambers. The report was short and not-so-sweet: Longinus had been executed.

"Very good," Pilate said. "And his gladius, were you able to fetch it for me?"

"It was already gone when I went to retrieve it."

"I figured as much. What a careless thing to do. That mentor of yours truly lost his mind. It's a curious thing. Your next assignment is unfortunately below your rank, but Caiaphas and his annoying friends insist I send a centurion and his best soldier to guard the Nazarene's tomb for a few days. Fears about people stealing his body or something like that. I want these people out of my face already. Find a good soldier and go. Men are waiting outside. They'll take you to Joseph of Arimathea, the tomb's owner."

Departing

Longinus and his son rode their horses for the next two days. They stopped a few times to eat and sleep. It was after dusk when they finally arrived at the Caesarean port.

"Where will we go?" his son asked.

"Home, my boy."

"Are your parents still alive?"

"My mother was when I left. I'm not sure now. It's been many years. I don't know about my father either. He left us when I was a bit older than you. We were not his permanent family, as my mother once told me. He was several years older than her and most likely had another family in Cappadocia, where he was from and probably still is if he's alive. I do have brothers and sisters. They'll all want to meet you. I have so many stories to tell them." Longinus knew the main story he'd tell was about the blood that healed his eye from the man who once rescued his son's mother from an angry mob.

He found a ship going to Syracuse, where his family still lived. The captain said he wasn't leaving till the festival was over. They would have to wait around until then. He provided food and allowed them to sleep on the ship if they agreed to help prepare for the journey.

The Festival of Unleavened Bread had ended when Simon and his family were ready to pack their carriage and head to the port in Caesarea, where his large ship had been docked this whole time, waiting for their return.

"But why must you leave so early?" Caleb asked. "So much has happened during your stay. Leah and I could use your company. You certainly need more rest. Not only this, but the sun is setting. At least wait till morning like everyone else."

"Brother, *too much* has happened," said Simon. "That's precisely why it's time to go. We've been here for months already. The roads will be crowded with all the extra travelers in the morning. I prefer to ride through the night. You know that. I also have some business to take care of."

"*Business*," Caleb repeated with delight. "It's good to see you coming back to your senses. I like the sound of that."

"*Personal* business," Simon clarified but without specification.

They said their goodbyes and embraced one last time. Simon held onto his brother a little longer than usual. He wasn't at all sure when or if he'd see him again. He didn't express this to Caleb, but it was on his heart and mind.

Before they exited the property, Joanna stared at the dirt once stained with Ethan's blood. She looked away and whispered to herself, "*People can only harm the body, but never the soul.*"

Alexander and Rufus were each on a horse, pretending they were soldiers in a battle. Caleb sent a few servants to go along with them to bring the horses, carriage, and supplies back. He also sent three newly hired guards to provide security.

The journey took about three days. When they arrived at the port, the ship's captain yelled, "Is it true? Has my master finally returned?"

Simon laughed and greeted the Greek man who had steered his large Alexandrian ship for years. He was as close to him as a brother and treated him like one.

"And what have you spent your time doing during my long absence...or should I not ask such embarrassing questions?"

"A little bit of this and a little bit of that," the captain said. "Not much else."

The port was already busy with countless Passover pilgrims leaving the festival to return to their homes.

While unloading one of the wagons, Simon clumsily bumped into something like a tree. He found himself on the ground. The sun was blotted out. A large hand reached out and helped him to his feet. Simon and Longinus recognized each other at once. How could Simon forget the face of the man who forced him to carry

Jesus's cross? He found it a curious thing to see the Roman's eye restored. They exchanged no words. Neither showed signs of malice. They both knew the recent events transformed them in unspeakable ways. No longer did they stare at one another as gentile or Jew, oppressor or subject. They were fellow travelers now. They briefly acknowledged one another with a nod and carried on with their separate journeys.

Barabbas and his family were also at the port that day, looking to board the first ship out to anywhere. He desired a place to start a new life. When Barabbas saw the large centurion who mysteriously spared his life—but barely—get on the ship to Syracuse, he turned around to hide his face. Barabbas then found another ship headed for Cilicia, which seemed far away enough from both Longinus and his old life as a Zealot. He wasn't sure what he'd do when he got there. Barabbas was a skilled carpenter by trade and his wife was a seamstress. They'd find their way.

Epilogue

Judas Iscariot returned the thirty pieces of silver he received for his betrayal. However, some transactions are nonrefundable. With a guilt-ridden conscience taunting him like a demon, he found a tree in a field and hanged himself.

Marcus knew what he experienced at the tomb of Jesus. That didn't stop him from accepting bribe money from Caiaphas and his secret council. Old habits don't break easily. But Marcus was never the same. Especially after he wasn't whipped for allowing Jesus's body to be stolen. He and the other soldier were asleep when it happened. That was the story he was to give Pilate and he gave it. Marcus assumed Pilate was also paid off to let it go because let it go, he did. Pilate listened and accepted the report without question.

But Marcus could *not* let it go. He felt his conscience burn with each false word he told the governor. Marcus was in a daze for weeks after that. The other soldier at the tomb left town without explanation. Marcus understood. The truth of what happened was far too great for a normal life to resume.

Marcus thought about the miraculous healing of his mentor's eye. He thought of Longinus declaring how Jesus must have been the Son of God. But most of all, he thought of his encounter at the tomb. What did he see? A demigod? What else could it have been? He had no idea. But it was large, powerful, and wrapped in lightning. He and his subordinate were frozen with fear at the sight of the impossible figure who removed the stone covering the tomb's entrance. Then it happened. Marcus saw it with his own two eyes. Jesus of Nazareth emerged from the grave's darkness, stooped to clear its threshold, stretched out his arms, yawned, and walked away. Both Romans saw and heard all that took place, but neither could speak nor move for an hour. Marcus was ruined. Everything changed.

It took less than thirty days. It became apparent the new centurion was unfit to perform his duties. Pilate gave Marcus a choice: be demoted to a common guard in Caesarea or patrol the streets of Jerusalem. He felt this second option was properly humiliating, assuming his subordinates disdained the Jews as much as he did and would not want to deal with them daily. Marcus still chose the latter. However, the demotion did not last long either.

When the morning of Pentecost came, Marcus was patrolling the streets of Jerusalem. A large crowd of Jewish worshippers from various regions were gathered. They were listening to a man preach about strange things: God pouring out his spirit on all people, young men seeing visions, old men dreaming dreams. Marcus hardly understood any of it but was captivated nonetheless. He was about to walk away when he heard the man mention Jesus of Nazareth. He froze when he heard how he was put to death with the help of wicked men nailing him to a cross. Though he wasn't the one who did the nailing, Marcus couldn't help but feel he was still one of those wicked men. He was cut to the heart. Then the man explained how God raised Jesus to life and how it was impossible for death to keep its hold on him.

Marcus stayed and listened to the rest of the sermon. Again, much of it eluded his understanding. There were references to Hebrew scriptures he knew nothing of. But something like a fire began to stir deep inside Marcus.

When the man ended his sermon with a call to repentance and baptism, Marcus pushed through the crowd to meet him. His name was Peter, a disciple of Jesus. Marcus told Peter about his experience at the crucifixion and the miraculous healing of his mentor's eye. He told him about the shining figure at the tomb and how guilty he felt about taking money to lie about it. He confessed every offensive thing he could remember saying or doing. He told Peter about Felix. He knew he put his friend out of his misery, but hated himself for doing it. Peter was astonished at the gentile's words. Marcus left after his confession.

Soon after this encounter, Marcus quit the Roman army and searched for Peter. He eventually got baptized, along with other gentiles who became followers of Jesus. He joined Peter and the other disciples in this new work of reconciling man to God.

Three years after Jesus was crucified, both Pontius Pilate and Joseph ben Caiaphas were deposed. Caiaphas for his collusion with the governor, Pilate for his unwarranted cruelty after slaughtering a group of what he called "trouble-making Samaritans" in a village near Mount Gerizim.

Caiaphas routinely made payments to the governor for various favors. This made Pilate not *completely* hate the high priest. Though it did make several in Jerusalem hate him. Separate complaints about them reached Rome. Pilate was sent to stand trial before the emperor and give an account for his unprovoked massacre.

He arrived in Rome just after Tiberius died of a heart attack. Pilate was then exiled to Gaul. The forced early retirement was a much-needed relief. Soon after Jesus was crucified, Pilate began to suffer from chronic nightmares. Each dream was the same. Pilate was pulled off his judgment seat and flogged severely. He was then dragged to Golgotha and nailed to a cross. Vultures swooped down from the dark sky to peck his flesh off bit by bit. Pilate often woke up screaming and in a cold sweat. It was a rare occasion when he slept through the night. His wife told him it was punishment for not listening to her. The once-governor was only at peace when he arose early in the morning to tend to his small grape vineyard.

However, his retirement was short-lived. Another man came into power by the name of Gaius Julius Caesar Augustus Germanicus, whom most simply referred to as Caligula. The new emperor recalled many exiled under Tiberius, including Pontius Pilate. Not trusting the new emperor's intentions and fearing the worst, Pilate refused to appear in Rome. Caligula was insulted and responded swiftly with an execution-by-suicide order. A detachment of soldiers was sent to oversee and finish the job if the order was met with resistance. It was not. Despite his wife's pleading to escape at the sight of soldiers marching up their hill, Pilate ignored her screams and waited for them, knowing full well what was to come. He drank the hemlock cocktail without fuss, cursed the new emperor, and died.

Caiaphas, on the other hand, never suffered from nightmares. He did, however, suffer a loss of public favor, as the people saw him for the corrupt politician he truly was, rather than the religious figure he pretended to be. The Council of Thirteen officially disbanded even before he was deposed, as members grew increasingly weary of the high priest's ulterior motives and hunger for power. And some of the members—particularly the sons of Annas—had ulterior motives of their own.

Due to his extreme wealth and established connections, Caiaphas remained part of Jerusalem's elite for the rest of his life. It was merely a formality and his influence was limited. Joseph ben Caiaphas was always invited to important engagements but was never again called upon for counsel.

Weeks after her son's crucifixion and burial, Hannah awoke earlier than usual to a man at the threshold of her home.

"Are you Hannah, the mother of Micah?" the man asked.

"He came to me first!" Ruth said, standing behind the man. She was nearly out of breath. "He said it's of great importance and that it's good news. That's the only reason I showed him where you live. Otherwise, I would've sent him away."

"It's fine," said Hannah. "I'm the one you seek. What do you want?"

The man led Hannah out of the threshold to see the large caravan taking up much of the road and stretching back farther than she could see. Several neighbors were already outside investigating the commotion.

"What's this all about?" she asked.

"My master has given me strict orders to transfer all of his wealth and possessions to you. It's far too much to list every item present. I know there is much silver, gold, spices, fine clothing, and various treasures from around the world. All of these servants will help you move into whatever home you desire."

Hannah fainted.

When she opened her eyes a few minutes later, she expected it to all have been a dream. But it was no dream. Hannah was suddenly wealthy.

Simon sent his best advisors and property managers to help Hannah get set up with her new life of luxury.

There was a small palace in Jerusalem's Upper City, not far from the homes of Caleb and Caiaphas. It was available for purchase after its owner died, an old rich man with no heirs. A price was negotiated and she moved in immediately, taking her neighbor Ruth along with her.

The high priest and his father-in-law came to greet the curious woman and give her a warm welcome. Hannah had never been treated with such respect, especially by men in powerful positions.

"If she'll be a friend of the temple treasury, she'll be a friend of ours," said Annas to Caiaphas after meeting Hannah for the first time.

"But where did she come from?" asked Caiaphas. "Where's her husband? Does she have sons? This is unheard of."

"No one seems to know much about her," Annas responded.

Having come into sudden wealth and the possession of massive quantities of various spices, Hannah entered the spice trade at once. Caleb took notice of his new neighbor and competitor. He did not recognize her as the poor widow whose son was buried in his garden. It was not until she came to visit the tomb that he learned it was indeed the same woman.

She must've pretended to be poor that day, he thought. What a strange thing to do. However, it finally made sense to him why his brother was friends with her.

Caleb eventually tried to partner up with Hannah, but she declined. She was doing fine and did not need a partner. She never learned of her son's criminal activities at Caleb's house that led to his arrest. Nor did Caleb ever learn Hannah's son was the very thief who held a blade to his niece's throat. That secret stayed with Simon and Dinah. The absence of this knowledge allowed Caleb and Leah to be good friends with Hannah for the rest of their lives.

As for Simon and Dinah, it turned out they were unable to rid themselves of all their wealth no matter how hard they tried. For even after they gave everything they had to Micah's mother—save the ship that carried it all, which Simon gave to his Greek captain as a token of appreciation for all his faithful years of service—more wealth would immediately enter the couple's life. The day after their Cyrene palace was sold and emptied of all its possessions, a man from the East came with a message from King Gondophares that read, "Your name is highly esteemed in my land and has been mentioned by some of my chief advisors. Please accept this humble gift for all your loyal years of business with my people."

This "humble" gift was a cart of gold and jewels from the king's massive treasury. Later that same day, three other men came to Simon to pay off their enormous outstanding debts.

The couple needed to find more poor people to bless. They consistently gave away everything that came to them, only keeping what they needed to live on. It soon became apparent it was impossible to out-give the Lord. But Simon and Dinah spent the rest of their lives trying to do just that. Even Caleb did not believe their story of giving everything away only to get more in return shortly after.

"At first, I thought you were crazy," Caleb said. "Now I think you're a liar." Despite being told plainly, Caleb never understood the secret of his brother's perpetual success. Nor of Hannah's, for that matter. However, he and Leah were very grateful Simon's family moved in with Hannah and Ruth after leaving Cyrene. Hannah was grateful for this as well. Her life was rich in more ways than one.

Simon and Dinah grew old enough to see two of their children marry and have children of their own. Alexander married the first daughter of Nicodemus, and Joanna married the captain of the Temple Guard. Rufus never married. Instead, he befriended the great apostle Paul during one of his stays in Jerusalem. He accompanied him on many journeys to spread the gospel of Jesus to both near and distant lands. Simon's family became known for taking care of the newly formed church.

Simon died wealthy despite his outrageous generosity. Dinah lived for another nine years after her husband passed. She continued to serve the followers of Jesus in Jerusalem for a while. Due to her son's deep friendship with Paul, she became like a second mother to the apostle and used her inexhaustible wealth to tend to his needs whenever he visited the city.

Eventually, Paul persuaded Rufus and Dinah to relocate to Rome. They stayed a few years and neither suffered martyrdom as Paul did at the hand of Nero. The emperor had conveniently blamed Christians for the Great Fire that burned down and destroyed many of the city's districts. Paul was beheaded on the same day Peter was crucified upside down. Rufus and Dinah narrowly escaped Nero's persecution program. They still managed to rescue several Christians and helped them establish residence in various regions both in and out of Roman jurisdiction.

Marcus was one of these people. He would have preferred prison and even death with Peter and the others. But the apostle urged him to go with Rufus and Dinah and carry on the work of the ministry elsewhere. Marcus settled in Damascus, where he assisted Ananias, the man who restored the sight of Paul after his conversion. During Marcus's free time, he amazed the city's children with his dagger-throwing skills. Even in his old age, Marcus could still hit a target's center from twenty steps away. When he wasn't talking about Jesus, he'd often tell stories about the centurion he once knew who could throw a dagger from the same distance and slice an apple in half as it rested on someone's head.

It was hard for the boy to watch. On their way to Syracuse, Longinus brought him to the upper deck to throw his gladius into the Ionian Sea.

"But Father, I was hoping you'd give that to me one day."

"There are certain things a father should not pass down to his son. The sword is one of them."

However, what Longinus *did* pass down to his son was a love for the sea. He taught him everything he knew. They caught sharks with harpoons and smaller fish with nets. Along with Longinus's nephews, they built a successful fishing business in only a few short years. They also hired local fishermen to operate a small fleet of boats.

But with each passing year, Longinus felt more and more the pull to leave it all. Business was good. His son was grown and able to handle all the responsibilities without guidance. It was time to let the boy go, for he was now a man.

Longinus had an experience with Jesus that never left his thoughts or heart. He formed the habit of retelling this experience to every new person he met. Whenever he told the story, people returned in the following days to tell him that Jesus appeared to them in dreams. Some said they were freed from a guilty conscience for offenses they committed. Others were given instructions about upcoming decisions they needed to make. Some even reported being healed from illnesses upon waking. Even in death, Jesus displays his power, Longinus thought. This inspired him to take his story to Cappadocia, where his father was from.

Though Longinus had prepared his heart over the years to let go of his son when the time came, his son made no such preparation to let go of his father. Nor did he suspect he would have to, as Longinus kept his intentions private. With many tears and mixed emotions, they said their final goodbyes. The mystery of his father's abrupt parting haunted the younger Longinus for quite some time after this.

Several years later, a ship arrived at the Syracuse port where the younger Longinus docked his fishing boats. Men stepped off and began telling the locals about Jesus of Nazareth. They were calling the people to believe in him for forgiveness of sins. Three of these individuals happened to be from Cappadocia.

Longinus told them he knew about the man they spoke of and asked how *they* knew about him. They told him the story of a monk who moved to Cappadocia a few years prior. This monk told everyone in their village how he was once a centurion who oversaw the execution of Jesus of Nazareth.

"The monk told us this Jesus was more like a god who miraculously healed his blindness!" the men said. "At first, we did not believe him. But then Jesus appeared to us in dreams and spoke true and powerful messages about our lives."

"And what became of this monk?" the young Longinus asked.

"The monk lives. He devotes most of his time to prayer and telling travelers his story. He is the most peaceful man we have ever known."

Longinus did not reveal he was the son of the monk they spoke of. But his heart was finally at rest. His father was well. The men asked if Longinus would like to join them on their missionary voyage but he declined. He had a long overdue journey of his own to make. It was one he never found the time for. Now that he knew his father was alive and there were family members and trustworthy fishermen able to run the business in his absence, the time had finally come.

The port at Caesarea was unusually crowded. Longinus rented donkeys from a man who would accompany him and his family to the outskirts of Jerusalem. There were many pilgrims on the road. The guide informed Longinus he had arrived just in time for Passover.

The inn looked almost the same as when he and his mother lived there thirty years earlier. The fig tree was still there and healthier than ever. The land had developed quite a bit. In front of the inn was a large vineyard. Longinus hoped he would find Nathan as an old man, still in his right mind. He tried not to cling to this hope too tightly, fearing he had already died a long time ago. However, not only was Nathan alive, he was working diligently in the vineyard. Others worked alongside him.

"You did it!" Longinus said with a laugh, recognizing him at once. "You got your vineyard."

Nathan, however, did not recognize the man standing before him, nor his booming voice, though both seemed familiar. He stared at the strange man and his family. It was not until Longinus said, "Dod," that he knew who it was. Nathan began to weep and walked over with his arms open to embrace the man who was once like a son to him.

"I thought I'd never see you again," said Nathan. "You're bigger than your father, you know? For a moment, I almost thought you were him. But those eyes...those eyes belong to your mother. And who is this small crowd you brought with you?"

Longinus introduced Nathan to his wife and children. Nathan had adult children as well, along with a few grandchildren.

"This one is my oldest daughter," said Nathan.

"And what is your name?" asked Longinus.

"Kezia," she answered.

Longinus smiled.

They celebrated Passover and stayed for several weeks. All the children played with one another. They spoke about what became of their lives. Their hearts and bellies were full.

Nathan's family took care of the vineyard, along with their neighbors. It was a joint venture. Nathan told how the community finally banded together to stop the abuses of the rogue tax collectors. They sold grapes and wine. As the years passed, they collectively increased their wealth little by little. Whenever the tax collectors tried to take more than what was owed, all the neighbors formed a mob outside the home where the abuse was taking place. That was the end of their financial tyranny.

As the sun set the day before Longinus and his family were to take to the seas and return home, Nathan brought him to a remote section of the vineyard. Nestled in a corner not far from the fig tree but away from its shade was a set of large decorative memorial stones. The sweet smell of crushed grapes hung in the air.

"This is where I buried your mother," Nathan said. "I come out here every morning before I get to work. I talk to God. I talk to her. Sometimes I sit still and say nothing."

Though tensions between the Romans and Jews had escalated over the years, neither Longinus nor Nathan knew what the near future held. Zealots would revolt against the Romans for the last time. Jerusalem would fall. The temple would be burned to the ground. Countless people would be displaced, enslaved, and killed. In a few hundred years, Rome too would fall. Kingdom after kingdom would continue to rise, fall, and be replaced by yet another. This was the way of the world.

But a new kingdom was now born. A kingdom that would never end. A kingdom from a different world. A kingdom of love. A kingdom of life. It resided in the hearts of its citizens, who were citizens by choice. This new kingdom had already waged war against the darkness. The day will come when it triumphs over it once and for all.

For now, the two men enjoyed their moment of tranquility. Longinus stared at the memorial stones and thought of his mother. Kezia was long gone, but she and her words lived eternally in his heart. He stooped to pick a red windflower. Goodness stirs beneath it all, no matter how barren a land may appear. Dead things get buried in the ground and are seemingly lost forever. But soon new growth emerges from the dark earth. Love always finds a way to conquer death.

ABOUT THE AUTHOR

Giancarlo Ghedini is an author, copywriter, and podcaster. He's written two novellas, one collection of short stories, and one nonfiction ebook. He's been featured in numerous magazines, publications, and short story anthologies. He's the creator and host of *The Story King Podcast* and *News on Knees | The Prayer Podcast*. Born and raised in New York, he now lives with his wife and three sons in Middle Tennessee.

Follow and Support:

https://linktr.ee/GiancarloGhedini

Darrin DeLuza and the Devil, Cain's Confession, and *Massimo's Mirror and Other Stories* are all available on Amazon.

www.ingramcontent.com/pod-product-compliance
Lightning Source LLC
LaVergne TN
LVHW041924070526
838199LV00051BA/2717